MANTIS

MANTIS

Mulhenney & Poole

Steve Zell

Steve Zell (signature)

Edited by Leigh Anne Beresford
Cover design & artwork, MANTIS © 2020 by Steven J. Pitzel

MANTIS   Mulhenney & Pool, Copyright © 2020 by Steve Zell.
All rights reserved.

Printed in the United States of America

First Printing March 2021
Tales From Zell, Inc. TM
Portland, Oregon

ISBN-13: 978-0-9847-4689-7

LCCN: 2021902810

Acknowledgements

Special thanks to Leigh Anne Beresford; editor, friend, and best 'cuz anyone could ever have - and to Dennis Hackin for those "are you writing?" emails.

Thank you, Douglas Spotted Eagle, for your ability to learn and teach anything that comes your way. You're an inspiration.

Also, thank you Billy – a man so talented and interesting even your old house in Bel Air gave me a plot device for this book...

And, of course, thank you, Nina, for all you do and have done through all of this.

Table of Contents

Chapter 1

Summer, 1968
Phoenix, Arizona

Deanne Mulhenney opened her eyes to a murky, blue haze. It was a dull ache that woke her. A throbbing in her left temple that was there and gone...and there it was again.

She brushed her sheets aside and sat, holding her head in her palms.

Deanne had left the sliding glass open to the desert before slipping away to a dream she couldn't quite remember now.

Somehow her feet found the floor.

She slouched before her bathroom sink, watching the clear, cool water slide from the brass and swirl, soundlessly, into the basin below. Her fingers slipped in, cupped that coolness toward her face.

The pretty, smooth-skinned brunette with plush red lips and deep, blue eyes, her key to opening countless doors in the notoriously hard-nosed world of investigative reporting, was nowhere to be seen.

The mirror before her framed nothing but a bright blue moon.

Deanne turned to see the flash of a small star.

She heard the shot just as her mirror shattered.

Los Angeles

The phone rang loudly on and on beside Sara Poole's bed. It would have woken her if she'd been there.

But right now the statuesque Sara stood on a balcony high above Hollywood Boulevard, staring down on the city lights with eyes as dark as the clove cigarette in her hand. Given the scents coming from the street, the sweet drag she pulled from that cigarette was more welcome, more calming, than ever. Still, it was a bad habit, just one of many she'd picked up lately. She could blame Deanne for putting her on that path, she supposed.

She grimaced and nearly snuffed out the thin cigarette on the balcony rail. But Sara was too tidy for that. It didn't take long to find an ashtray.

"I...don't do this...often." The woman was sweet-faced and voluptuous, thirty-two at most. The missing wedding ring had left an indent in her finger – underscored by a bright pink tan line. Sara hadn't missed that. And she hadn't cared.

Sara nodded.

"Of course you don't. It's not a problem."

-=-.=-.=-.=-

"Good morning, Sunshine." Ben chirped. "How's it hanging?"

However he did it, whatever amount of caffeine it took, the twerp always came to work wide awake. Too wide awake. This morning had come way too fast for Sara. The ripeness of the bloated customer on the table, an obvious *floater* – literally a body discovered floating in water, didn't help.

"Left today, and yours?"

"Straight down the middle."

"Huh, always figured you for a banana. Kinda' bent."

Off-putting at first, Sara had come to expect the boy's-room talk from Ben, had eventually come to enjoy the back-and-forth. In the male world of forensic pathology, the tanned and tall, dark-haired beauty – a girl whose expectations from parents and friends had placed her somewhere between Olympic diving champion and fashion model – was an oddity to say the least. In this world, locker talk was simply one more subject to be mastered.

"So where'd they pull this one from?"

"Ivanhoe."

Ivanhoe was the upper of two small lakes that made up the Silver Lake reservoir system, the lower being Silver Lake itself. Not much more than a spillway separated the two.

A young woman, her blue-gray flesh swollen and torn, lay on the table before them. The first responders had done their best to keep her intact, but the combination of water, summer heat and bacteria had made their job damn near impossible. Water, the best overall if not truly universal solvent was an amazing equalizer. Had she been beautiful in life, plain? Whatever she'd been, she wasn't now.

For a moment, the ruptured face took on the face of last night's sweet-faced, hook-up; that face melted into the handsome, no-nonsense but fatally naive face of Sondra Tucker. Sondra was one player in a campaign of murder Sara and her friend, Investigative Reporter, Deanne Mulhenney, had investigated in Arizona. Sondra had become a victim herself, the only floater Sara had actually met before death.

"You need a minute?" Ben actually looked concerned.

"I'm fine. Let's turn her...very, very carefully."

At day's end Sara pulled her scrubs and gloves, and dropped them into their appropriate bins as she had a thousand times before.

She stepped out into the bright sunlight feeling happier than ever the ocean was only a two-minute, no-sweat jaunt from her rental in Hermosa Beach. She'd be walking that trail soon enough. Just one more bit of business before –

"Want to get a drink?"

Sara was surprised to see Ben behind her. Not just because he had never followed her out of the Crime Lab before, because she honestly hadn't heard him, hadn't been aware of him at all.

Her mouth began to form the word, "no" before her brain even engaged.

She surprised herself when she switched gears and said,

"Not tonight."

It was still too harsh. The kid, with no height to spare, visually shrank. *Crap, why do I care?*

Because you do.

"Class tonight," she explained. "Got plans tomorrow?"

He didn't have to answer that; she was pretty sure he didn't.

"Uh, I don't think so."

She nodded, "let's do it."

Two hours later, wrapped in her sweat-soaked *gi* and feeling the strength of smooth hardwood beneath her feet, she faced the *makiwara;* stance balanced and sure, fists upturned at her waist.

She screamed the *kiai* as she lashed out, rapidly screwing her striking fist upright, wrist ramrod straight, as she cocked the other back. She landed punch after powerful punch, the deadly straight punch they call *chokuzuki.* What stood before her was not the padded wood makiwara, but the vulnerable center point just below a man's rib cage; the notch of his sternum.

Utterly drained, breathing fire and no longer able to lift her arms; Sara rested.

She began again.

-=-=-=-=-

"Hard day at the office, mister?"

Barely aware the bartender had returned, the man in the Brioni suit tapped the half-empty glass beside him with his cigarette hand, a few ashes drifted onto the ice. He didn't notice.

"Yeah, sure. Hard day."

The man took another draw from his cigarette.

Had it been? Sure it had. He was the fourth in line creative at an agency that barely had room for one. Cutthroat didn't say it; and today, his cherry campaign had been dragged out and shot down by number two. So what? Life wasn't fair. Right now something else held his attention.

Shiny, meticulously coiffed raven-hair cut straight across her forehead – bobbed at the sides like an Egyptian princess. Her skin was a porcelain smooth cream, she had wide, ruby lips and sculpted, long smooth legs she wasn't too shy to show. The woman was dressed for someplace else – someplace much better than this.

She'd been giving him the eye ever since he noticed her.

But she wasn't alone.

And that was maybe the *unfairest* unfair of all.

Nebbish was the first word that came to mind.

Here she was, a Lamborghini in the Ford showroom – and *that* sat across from her.

Baby-round head with a bald pate only a monk would be proud of; thick glasses. Even with his heels pulled up tight the troll's toes barely tapped the floor below.

The man in the suit shook his head as a fresh Manhattan clacked down beside the ashtray. He wall-eyed it, feeling the first two now.

"Not fair is it?"

The bartender had read his mind, cloudy as it was. What had she said her name was? Lucy? Lucille? He couldn't remember. She smiled. Not bad looking herself. Blonde, fresh-faced. Nebraska came to mind. He'd barely noticed her before. But now…

Now…he was definitely feeling the drinks.

Time to go.

He downed the Manhattan in two long gulps, chomped the maraschino cherry and spat out the stem. He fumbled for his wallet.

Two bills drifted to the floor. He reached down – and saw long, silky legs.

He followed them up to the Lamborghini's blue eyes.

"Come join us," she purred.

-=-.=-.=-.=-

Just off the Pacific Coast Highway in Malibu, the home of movie stars and those wealthy enough to be neighbors of movie stars, the rocky outcrop of Point Dume overlooks a spectacular view of endless ocean, and pristine, secluded beaches. Only a few months earlier, a film crew had wrapped the final scene of the science fiction drama, *Planet of the Apes,* on this very spot.

In the deep blue early hours of morning, the end of a very different drama was playing out.

Some five hours after the man in the Brioni suit had tasted his last Manhattan, the nebbish stopped for a rest.

Dragging this particular load was no easy task. But, as with many jobs he'd been given, he performed this one diligently, without question. It had to be done.

At cliff's edge, he unzipped the long garment bag and rolled its heavy contents over the side.

Moments later, the green panel truck he'd parked nearby took him home.

Chapter 2

Well, this was a mistake.

Sara didn't even drink beer. But, here she was with her partner in dissection, nursing one.

A young couple in jeans and flowered shirts harmonized, more or less, from the smoky corner of the bar – some song about Vietnam and President Johnson which they seemed to be making up on the fly.

Ben was nodding to some rhythm only he could find in their music.

"You come here a lot?" She asked, finally.

"No."

She laughed. "Okay. So...any reason we're here?"

He shook his head.

"I just thought. I dunno. You know, we work together every day – and outside of insulting each other – we never really talk."

"Thought you liked the banter."

He smiled. A real smile.

"Well, yeah. But...we don't really know each other."

Oh no, here it comes. The sudden tightness in her shoulders, her temples – the shield against male expectations quickly dropping into place. She was pretty, she knew that, but to a man that meant –

"It's not like that," he said, feeling her discomfort.

"Oh."

"I mean, you're attractive – I mean, really attractive. I mean – you're smoking hot."

"Okay, I get it. You have really got to work on your small talk. Did you bring me out here to tell me you're homosexual?"

He stared at her blankly.

"No," he winced, "uh. I mean." He shook his head. "No, that's not why I wanted to...talk, what I wanted to say. It's you. You're not the same. It's the FBI. What happened to you in Arizona?"

She raised her hand to the passing bartender.

"We need two shots of Jack here."

"You got it."

"We have to work tomorrow," Ben reminded her.

"How bad do you want to know?"

Ben took a deep breath, wide-eyed as the glasses struck the bar between them.

Sara raised hers and Ben, grudgingly, did the same.

"To the dead..." She toasted, "...and lots of 'em."

Ben choked on his. Tears of raw-throated pain burst over his flushed cheeks.

"Let's go somewhere we can talk," she said.

Ben slid uneasily off the stool, scanning for an empty booth. He picked up his half-empty beer.

Sara dropped two bills on the counter.

"Not here. Suck that down. I know a place. It's not far."

If Ben's eyes were wide before, they were dinner plates now. A trip to *P. Willows* was obviously more than he'd bargained for tonight. The West-Hollywood basement bar, one you entered from a back-alley with nothing but a neon pink Siamese cat sitting in a tree buzzing over the stairway, was a naughty secret to anyone who knew.

One year ago the Haight-Ashbury district of San Francisco may have ushered in a Summer of Love but one summer later all the free love was decidedly straight love. For other persuasions some things were still better left unsaid.

Poor boy, Sara thought as they negotiated the phalanx of business-suit bulls toying with their party-dressed lipsticks. Most ignored the two of them; the few evil eyes cast their way quickly withered with a smile from Sara; they turned back to the business of each other.

She led him to a booth in the deep recesses.

"Your usual, Traci?" The slim waitress, her full lips painted to match her fire-engine red wig, leaned in for a quick peck on the cheek, giving Ben a clear shot of low-hanging but definitely forbidden fruit.

Sara considered the intestinal mix… She shook her head.

"Shot of Jack, Flame."

"And what's she having?"

"The same."

Ben frowned as Flame retreated to the bar.

"I really resent that -"

"It's for your protection. Be cool. You're in unfriendly territory."

"Then why did you bring me here? And what's with Traci?"

"You can be anyone you want here and it stays here. Nobody really knows anyone. No better place to talk."

Ben considered that. Finally, he nodded.

"What happened in Phoenix? You were supposed to be on vacation. Why are the Feds in our lab? Where's our evidence from Alice and Dinkens?"

Sara downed the shot before it had time to hit the table. Ben held his.

Her trip to Phoenix, Arizona, was never going to be a vacation, but she had told Ben it was. She'd really driven there to connect the dots between two victims she and Ben had autopsied here in LA – the ones Ben referred to as "Alice and Dinkens," and two similar cases she'd read about in Phoenix. Four men – yes, Alice was a man – all victims, roughly the same age, had died within days of each other. All four were born in Phoenix and all four had drowned. The real kicker was that only one death happened anywhere near enough water to drown a rat let alone a grown man.

Sara had come back with enough evidence to convict in those and three other murders, including a fifteen-year-old cold case. She and Deanne had conducted a career investigation for any team of detectives – let alone one reporter and an assistant medical examiner.

And that…was only part of the story. She'd left with so much more - secrets under seal she was legally bound never to tell anyone, let alone a fellow assistant medical examiner…and a broken heart.

Yeah, there was that…

"Okay…this is what I can tell you…"

9

And what she could tell him wasn't much, certainly not enough to satisfy him. She told him about Deanne Mulhenney, the reporter who'd written the article that brought Sara to Phoenix in the first place – a story that tied the two mysterious deaths she and Ben had worked to others in Phoenix. In the story she gave Ben, Deanne had become her partner in solving those murders, and a fifteen-year old cold case, nothing more. She mentioned Tahoma, the young Navajo man they called Tommy Red Hawk – but Sara left out his strange powers, the fact that he'd saved her life and Deanne's, and that he was, in fact, a multiple murderer. In this version of the truth, Tahoma was simply a witness in the cold case.

The rest of the story, the scandalous ending of a promising Senatorial campaign, was a tawdry tabloid feature now...and that nonsense would eventually burn out, as would the sham federal investigation into the disappearance of the would-be Senator's wife. That investigation had resulted in the confiscation and sealing of all related evidence by the FBI – including every bit of evidence and records from the autopsies she and Ben had performed.

The story Sara told wasn't enough for Ben, but it would have to do for now.

Bless me father, for I have sinned.

Deanne had forced Sara to say those words, to confess to Deanne's Catholic priest cousin what all of them knew – exactly what they had done to solve those murders – to bind her cousin to silence.

But there would be no such blessing here.

Ben took what she gave him for now. Jack Daniels helped.

"Fuck the FBI," he said, finally. "Where's...the men's room?"

"Hah!" She snorted. "Good luck with that."

A short time later, arm and arm for stability – they carried each other up the stairway from P. Willows. Ben, not exactly a deeply tanned denizen of the beach as Sara was in the first place, looked nearly translucent.

Sara could only imagine what he'd seen in that bathroom.

"You gonna make it home okay?"

He only nodded.

She was a little mad at herself now. Sure, she'd taken him to a place where no one cared if they talked shop or anything else – but it didn't have to be here. She'd done that on purpose, to tweak him a little.

Ben knew she was a lesbian – or at least suspected it. Half of his workplace banter consisted of homophobic insults. But this was reckless. It wasn't something you shouted to the world, let alone a coworker – even one who more or less knew.

She smelled and heard the boys before she saw them.

"Well isn't that sweet?" One of them said.

Two young drunks. She nearly took Ben back down the steps, but he pressed on.

"Whas' sa problem?" Ben said.

"Ignore them."

Things like this happened. P. Willows wasn't as well-kept a secret as it maybe should have been. Most straights who knew what it was just avoided it – but every now and then there were assholes, college boys more often than not, who got a kick out of hassling the women in suits; and two of them – one, tall and lanky, the other big and beefy – stood in their way.

She diverted Ben past, but the lanky one stepped sideways and nearly knocked Ben over.

"Hey...what the fuck, man?"

"Enjoy the night, boys," Sara said.

The other stepped in her way.

"We're just having fun."

"Good for you. But you're pretty much in the way again."

The assholes didn't move.

"So...which one of you is the girl?" The lanky one said.

"Which one of you fucking took biology?" Ben said.

The two glanced dumbly at each other, then one cocked his fist and the night slowed to a crawl.

Before that fist came within ten inches of Ben, Sara caught it by the wrist; her elbow slammed into the boy's cheekbone. The pop was so loud it nearly covered his shriek.

The beefy one lurched toward her. Her fist drove through his sternum. Her knee blasted his chin on his way to the pavement and something wet flew by her ear. He landed flat on his back, babbling, spitting blood and teeth.

11

"Move!" She yanked Ben forward. "Now!"

"What the fuck!"

They stumbled, then ran into the night.

They didn't stop for a breath until they'd reached Ben's car.

"What the fuck are you?" He coughed.

She wiped a red blob from Ben's cheek. It was the tip of the beefy boy's tongue.

"I'm the girl," she said.

Chapter 3

Hermosa Beach, CA
7:00 AM

The little boy prodded it with a long, thin chunk of driftwood.

He covered his eyes and ran a few feet back up the beach when flies rose up and swarmed him. Ralphie, a terrier who wouldn't take "no" for an answer, stopped barking just long enough to snap a couple mouthfuls of the annoying pests; coughing them back into the sand in bubbling, black-dotted gouts.

Netted in brown kelp, the odd, blue-gray log – odd, because it seemed to have four trunks joined at the middle like the letter X – slid forward as a new wave surged forward with a sound like steam.

Troy had been dutifully learning the alphabet and X was one of his favorite letters because it looked something like a cheerleader jumping up in the air, and he really liked football and the Los Angeles Rams.

"Leave that alone, Troy. Did you find any sand dollars?" His mom asked, corralling the rambunctious Ralphie.

Troy shook his head.

"X!" He announced proudly, pointing his stick at the bundle.

Then a bigger wave caught it, rolling the odd log halfway out of the kelp.

His mom vomited before she screamed.

Sara awoke from a terrible dream.

A flash from childhood, the high dive. She sprang backwards into the air. Only blue sky and seagulls when she'd climbed the ladder but the sky she saw now was black with thunderclouds.

She made a quick tuck and drop toward the safety of the deep pool below.

But there was no pool below her.

The phone rang again. Sara blinked. The first ring had broken the dream. Her head was so scrambled right now she'd forgotten.

She knocked the phone off her nightstand but caught the receiver. Her heart thundered in her chest.

Sara heard waves rolling as the first rays of a Saturday morning filtered through her blinds.

"Sara?"

"Deanne!"

"You okay? Sorry to call so early."

"*No problemo.* Good to hear your voice. Bad dream...I think. It's pretty much gone now."

"You and me both."

"Gonna take you into the kitchen." Which was a laugh, the kitchen in the more-than-modest house she rented was more of a nook with a sink, a box-like refrigerator most college dorm rooms wouldn't be that proud of, and a two burner stove with a coffee pot. The extra-long cord on her phone didn't have to travel all that far to reach it.

"You still having that dream?"

Sara knew that dream well. It came from one of the pieces of her story with Deanne she could never tell Ben. A sniper who'd been shadowing them for days took out one of the suspects Deanne was interviewing – shot the woman dead right in front of her. Sometime that same evening...the sniper left Deanne a gift. He'd placed a bullet on her dashboard, a sweet little reminder that he was still out there.

The truth of it was – that night hadn't been much better for Sara. A night of horrors for the both of them.

"Yeah, still having it, but not last night. I just wanted to...catch up."

Sara nodded as if Deanne could see her. She rinsed the basket, scooped the coffee grounds in, and, thankfully, the magic of percolation began.

"I'm glad you did. I'm sorry...I haven't been better at that."

"No...I understand. I miss you though."

14

"Miss you too."

And catch up they did. Deanne had gotten her old job back at the Arizona Tribune and a promotion for her part in solving what had been publicly called the Lily Murders. Nice rewards – but the truth was they were little more than consolation prizes given for tanking the real story. The real story, the one Deanne and Sara privately referred to as True Creature, had been scrubbed, sanitized, and ultimately buried.

Sara didn't have any good news to add from her side. They had a laugh about Sara's night out with her lab partner earlier in the week – Sara didn't mention it had ended in violence and bloodshed. None of that would have made Deanne feel any better about anything.

Sara did mention, somewhat sardonically, that Ben's tone in the lab had changed since their night out. He was even somewhat...respectful these days.

"Hold on, for a sec..."

A tiny garden and a public walkway fronted her tiny, stucco house. For a Saturday morning, there was an unusually loud hubbub of foot-traffic and voices outside. She reeled open her blinds to see doors swinging open across the way, her neighbors running toward the beach.

Then, the wail of an approaching patrol car.

"Deanne, something's going on. Call you back, 'kay?"

"Sara Poole, LA County –"

"Whoa surfer girl –"

A bright flash of the other night came to Sara; the last time a young man had stood in her way. Sara smiled at the fresh-faced cop.

"She's family, Willie. County Crime Lab. Let her through."

Detective Rick Cromwell, his black, wavy-hair blowing lightly above his sunglasses, tie tucked into his shirt to keep it from flapping in the sea breeze, waved her forward. But for the bolt of a scar crossing his chin the sun never seemed to reach, even Sara had to admit the guy was movie-idol perfect – maybe the one guy she'd ever consider... Even now as he crouched next to the monstrosity on the beach.

A few yards away, two rookie cops, soaking wet and visibly shaken, bent at the waist over a pile of driftwood. A tortuous trail of deep, frantic footprints and broken kelp lay in the path they must have taken lifting him away from the onrushing tide.

She felt for them. At their best, floaters were a horrid mess. But this one…this was a horrid bluish statue of stumps. Headless, its limbs ended in jagged tears at the wrists and ankles where marine life had begun finishing up someone else's work.

"Pro job." Rick said.

"Looks that way – someone really didn't want him ID'd."

The body lay on its left side just where the officers had left it. Two long exit wounds through the back. Machete? The signature was wide enough. The cuts were nearly mirror-image; one through each lung thrust with enough force to sever ribs, a blue gray flap of lung tissue hung from the left one. Powerful and vicious. Sara shook her head.

"They find anything with him?"

"Just the kelp and, well, he managed to keep *that.*"

Rick pointed his chin to the front side of the corpse, a sideways pyramid of brown kelp at the man's waist – yes, this was definitely a man's body. The end of a pink torpedo protruded from beneath the rubbery brown leaves. Under any other circumstance, it might have been comical.

"That what I think it is?"

"You're the doc," somehow he managed a wry smile.

The fact an easy target like privates had been overlooked by hungry marine predators was a minor miracle.

A very, very distraught woman, roughly Sara's age sat in the sand with a small child, shaded by a phalanx of officers.

"God. They found him?"

Rick nodded.

She headed toward the stricken mother and son. It was very possible they had seen something at first glance the others had missed, something that may have washed back into the Pacific before the officers had arrived.

She could offer some sort of comfort. She was a woman after all. Surely Sara's female face would be a welcome sight.

But she took one look at the blankness in the woman's eyes, her child's face buried deep into her side, a little boy unable to look in the direction of the thing on the beach – unlikely to see a beach the same way ever again.

16

A life-changing event for him. Sara knew those all too well.

What would she tell the kid? It's a movie prop, it isn't real? Enjoy your day?

You're a fucking forensic pathologist. Anything you say to these people will be wrong.

She turned back.

Rick stood up when she returned, pocketing his sunglasses for now. Deep gray, thoughtful eyes regarded her.

"Would like to say it's good to see you away from the office," he said.

Sara nodded, "Can't say we should do this more often."

"Any idea who'll be on this?" He asked.

"Likely Cross or Simpson."

He nodded, "they're good." He said it, but his eyes clearly showed he didn't mean it.

Sara held up her hands and backed away.

"I'm just here for the beach today," She said before she turned and walked back to her little bungalow off the Hermosa Beach Strand.

_=.=.=.=-

Deanne Mulhenney clacked away on her beast of a typewriter, a fresh Bloody Mary and a sweating glass pitcher of refills within easy reach.

The Arizona sun had already painted the steep rocks behind her house and the desert below a bright gold, but the air was still a Phoenix-cool 80 degrees. Downright frigid for these parts in the summer.

There were problems, real problems in the Maricopa County Medical Examiner's office. The Examiner himself had practically barricaded himself away midst rumors of corruption and mismanagement of the office.

As much as Deanne couldn't keep herself from a good corruption story – she wouldn't have touched anything involving autopsies and forensic pathology with a dead ocotillo branch before meeting Sara Poole.

Things had definitely changed...

When the phone rang, she almost didn't answer it.

"Deanne Mulhenney."

"Sara Poole," Sara laughed from the other end. If any interruption could have been pleasant – this was it.

"Did that sound too professional?"

"For Saturday, yes."

"It's been far too long...Miss Poole, did you say?"

"Nearly an hour. And, yes, this is Miss Sara Poole."

"To what do I owe the pleasure of this call? I'm a busy, busy woman."

"I can tell – I hear the ice clinking in your glass."

Deanne regarded her drink. She took a loud sip.

"Come over and I'll make another pitcher."

"I don't know, the waves are breaking really nice this morning, you should grab your board and drop by. Hey, I hear you do investigative reporting sometimes."

"I've been known to. Is this about the commotion outside your door?"

"A body washed up a half-mile up the beach. It happens. But this one was particularly gruesome, and peculiar. No hands, feet...or head."

"I'm so sorry. That...had to be awful."

"I've seen worse."

Deanne took that in. Even with the horrors she and Sara had been through on their investigation...the things Sara must come across daily in her work.... Sara was a different kind of animal. There was an awful twinge in Deanne's chest. Not from something she'd seen – but from something horrible she'd heard not long ago. She had been hiding, cowering from a killer, while the cold, systematic dismemberment of a woman's body happened only a few feet away. A woman she'd been speaking to only moments before...

"Tough thing was," Sara continued, "a little kid and his mom found it."

Deanne exhaled, loudly, it felt like a piece of her soul left with the breath.

"God, Sara. Are you going to have to...do the autopsy?"

"No. Well, not likely anyway. But it looks like a professional job, something like what happened...when you were in Piñon Rim. I know your feelings are still pretty raw on that one..."

To say the least.

"But would you do some checking?"
Deanne nodded.
"I'll see what I can find."
"Thanks, and..."
"What?"
"Nothing. That's it."
"Okay. Take care of yourself."
"Always."

Deanne hung the phone back on her kitchen wall. What was it Sara didn't say? An admonition for Deanne's continued drinking? Another invitation to visit her in California, to take a real vacation?

Their calls always made Deanne feel good at first, and left her feeling just a little empty.

Kachina dolls grimaced angrily with painted faces from her mantle in the den.

She finished her drink in one swallow.

Bodies sans hands, feet and head. How often did that happen?

She had some checking to do – the Tribune and Gazette news archives, the microfiche records at the library.

Before she did any of that, she made a call to her best friend – Sergeant, Bill Henry of the Phoenix Police Department.

Culiacán, Sinaloa, Mexico

Vin needed to relax, to take the edge off. The adrenaline was rushing, pounding inside him, making him wild. He couldn't afford to run wild now. He had to slow down, to ease up, play it natural and easy.

It had gone, as they say, like clockwork.

The payoff would be huge. He would be set for life.

A small packet of pure white crystals lay on the table.

No. No. No....don't do this now. Do not do this, Vin.

He had taken a cold shower, then a warm one, then hot. And now he sat, naked but for a robe, at the edge of a wide bed in a gigantic, gilded bedroom a boy of his humble beginnings could never have dreamed of.

Even as he clicked the white rocks onto the mirror, even as he drew the razor from its case and began chopping it like a pro chef info fine white powder, he told himself "no!"

Tomorrow morning he'd board a plane headed home to New York. He'd take his place at the table with his guys as if this little side-trip, this deal, had never taken place, and no one would be the wiser.

For now, he couldn't leave the villa. Tonight, Vin was the honored guest. The hospitality of the Don Guerrero could not be refused.

He had to remain calm, and this was no way to remain calm.

And still he chopped. He rolled a bill into a tube and sucked the burn into one nostril, then the next.

Aaaahh!! Hell, enjoy this. You are about to be the king! The king does what he wants...

A light knock at the door, expected though it was, nearly sent the mirror spinning when his knee struck it. A feel of warm liquid high in his sinuses. A single red dot splashed the mirror; he rubbed it into the powder before swiping it over his gums.

"Come in."

A fat, dwarfish servant pushed a silver serving cart into the room.

"I've already eaten."

"Compliments of the Don."

Vin was expecting a meal of another kind.

And then she appeared.

Her short silk robe led to long, smooth legs, and between those legs would be the meal Vin craved. Black hair as silken as her robe, cropped in front, bobbed at the sides...and *that mouth*. Her lips were full, dark cherries, voluptuous.

"Don Guerrero thought a massage might help you sleep," she purred. "Shall I try?"

"Fuck the massage. Bring me that mouth."

She smiled and let the robe drop to the carpet.

She pushed his robe from his shoulders and straddled him.

"Come on, now...is that all you've got?" A low, guttural whisper. She bit him lightly on the ear. It stung in a good way.

20

"I'll show you what I've got, bitch."

He swung her onto the bed...and what he had, suddenly, surprised even him. He impaled her, feeling every bit the man, every bit the king he was meant to be.

"Oh," she moaned, "that's it, that's what I want."

"I give a shit what you want."

"Then give me what you have."

She pounded her hips down onto him, covered his mouth with hers, and bit him again.

"Everything you have."

"Ah! You bitch!"

But even as he said it, he knew it felt good, felt better than anything he'd ever felt before. Heat poured through him, his own heat shot into hers...and kept coming.

She purred, and bit him again, on the cheek this time.

"Ah, ha, ha..."

The sting wasn't nearly as bad this time. He laughed, it actually felt good. So good.

And still, he kept coming. His penis wasn't just hard...it was hard as stone, the center of all his sensation now.

He saw her perfect breasts, her narrow waist, her beautiful pumping hips, a fleeting moment of fear as somehow...he realized he was losing sense of everything else.

She reached to the serving table, then slipped a thick rubber band onto one of his wrists, then the other. She pulled his ankles up behind her, slipped bands over each of them.

And even as he lost all other sensation, all other control, he felt the wonderful heat of his manhood in her, he never stopped thrusting it into her.

She leaned in to kiss his mouth again...but he couldn't feel her kiss...couldn't feel it at all.

A wet tearing sound. His vision doubled, her lips doubled...no...

She had torn his lips from him, she gobbled them down.

He felt himself screaming, heard himself screaming. But no sound left his throat.

And still...it felt so good.

She pulled one of his numb hands to her bloody mouth, uncurled two fingers and sucked them between those perfect lips.

They came away as strings of clean bones and ligaments.

And still she pounded him, and still he thrust himself back into her, blood squirted from her mouth, spattered those perfect breasts.

And he didn't care...didn't care at all.

It felt so good.

Until the last band slid tightly over his throat.

Without missing a beat in her dance of death, the woman removed the cover from the serving tray beside her. She produced two thick blades; they twirled in her hands and came to a stop against the smooth flesh of her forearms.

She reared back, blades folded before her as if in prayer, then plunged them through his chest.

A moment later the blades twirled in her hands once more; they stopped only when she crossed them at his neck.

Her scream was pure ecstasy as she ripped the blades away.

The room spun.

The last thing Vin saw was the fine marble tile of the floor.

Chapter 4

"What do you think, Pat?"

Deanne's cousin, Father Patrick Mulhenney, grimaced and shook his head.

The gruesome crime photos spread across her wrought iron table were a horrifying contrast to the beautiful calm of early evening.

Deanne and Father Pat sat cooled by the purple shadows of the mountain wall just behind Deanne's porch. The rosy glow of a spectacular Arizona sunset crept across the desert below.

"I still think you'd have been better off with a cat."

He was referring to Sara, of course. *"Get a pet,"* the accepted "remedy" for women living alone, had been Pat's constant refrain since her divorce...and then Sara had appeared on the scene.

"These aren't from Sara," she scoffed. "They're from Bill. What do you see?"

"What I *don't* see are heads, hands, or feet."

Deanne nodded, "Stick to what's there."

"Well, I'm not a forensics expert like your friend," he moved two of the photos together, a front and back shot of one of the victims. Then slid another pair beside the first. Both victims had what appeared to be bullet wounds to the upper chest – smallish holes at the pectorals and much larger, tearing wounds through their backs where the bullets had exited. "But I'd say these two – and at least two of the others here were shot to death and butchered later – I'm guessing to make them hard to identify."

"Yeah. Shot, then cut up. Some of them look like they'd been tortured first – but gunshots of one kind or another seem to have ended them."

"Evil," Pat said. "Hard to believe one human being can do this to another."

"Agree."

"These aren't local are they?"

"Two of them are. They found this one south of Sierra Vista, that one just outside of Tucson. The others are coastal. New Jersey, Florida, San Diego."

"It's common to find bodies like this?"

Deanne shook her head.

"Apparently it's getting that way. Bill said the coastal killings were Mafia hits. They traced the two Arizona murders to drug gangs from Mexico."

"Drug gangs?"

"Supposedly getting drugs across the border is becoming a big business now. Gangs are making a lot of money doing it."

"Jets and Sharks..." He was referring to the movie musical, *West Side Story*, from a few years back in 1961.

"But probably not as nicely dressed – and, as I recall, the weapon of choice with those gangs was a knife, not a gun. Sara made a point of saying her victim was stabbed to death; a big carving knife or a machete. He wasn't shot."

Pat shook his head, gravely.

"You sure you want to poke this bear? Look at these photos."

The photos carefully laid out around her sweating pitcher of margaritas were hideous. Beyond the decapitations, the torsos cried of the torture of cigar burns and deep gouges where pieces of flesh had been torn from the bone – likely with pliers.

"Deanne, the people who did this are brutal, inhuman."

Deanne sipped her margarita. An image came to her of a pretty, young woman sitting before her on a blanket beside a small campfire. Casually sipping Cabernet, the woman bragged casually on, describing her own part in a murder – until a bullet ripped through her; a bullet that came without warning, without sound, from somewhere, someone unseen.

Deanne could still feel the scrape of the rocks that chewed into her knees and forearms as she'd scrambled frantically to cover...

"It's a dangerous world, Pat."

-=-=-=-=-

New York City

As the old man tripped and lurched forward, a dark, slight young man seemed to reach out from behind him to help. In the everyday hustle of bodies moving north and south along the street, it was little more disruptive than a hiccup in a crowd of screaming fans. A break in the normal motion of things, a misdirection in the controlled chaos of street vendors, businessmen and women on their way to their jobs and tourists rushing to the next site.

The old man continued forward, but haltingly now, the small bag he carried dropped to the street before him. Pastries shattered against the concrete as he dropped to his knees. He coughed a gout of blood across the sidewalk.

Only then did the screams come, and suddenly the controlled chaos broke into pandemonium.

A few yards south, the doors of a parked but running sedan flew open. Four big men exited and ran toward the stricken old man, shouting, sending bodies tumbling out of their way.

"There was a dark young man!" someone shouted, "I don't see him now."

The dark young man moved with calm precision through a street that had gone helter-skelter, his footsteps balanced, sure and smooth as a dancer across a ballroom floor.

He entered the hotel lobby as tourists rushed out the door to see the cause of the commotion. Others looked up quickly from their coffee and newspapers as the wave of awareness of something important and possibly dangerous in the streets reached them.

He stopped for a moment a few feet from the door of the women's room, listening. A moment later, satisfied it was empty, he slipped easily inside, turned and locked it, jamming a wedge of steel between the frame and door for good measure.

He flushed away the thin gloves and bloody gauze.

The man moved quickly but surely. He unscrewed the small bolts from the air vent, pulled a small travel bag from the duct and quickly replaced the grate.

The image in the mirror was that of a slight, olive-skinned man with just a hint of whisker on his cheeks and chin. He pulled his turtleneck down, grasped the edge of his skin where olive broke abruptly to white, and tore the stubbled, colored latex upward and away to show the porcelain smooth chin and cheeks beneath.

He popped out the dark contact lenses, pulled away the lashes and brows, then withdrew a small jar of face cream from the bag. He smoothed the remaining color from his eyelids.

The face in the mirror was no face at all; a featureless, white mannequin looked back at him. A blank armature waiting for an artist's touch to bring it life.

Alienígena. Aliena.

That was her, what the other children had called her. The alien.

A bastardization of her real name, Alena.

But worse names would come.

"They are jealous, because you are perfect, because you can be whatever you want to be." Her father had tried so many times to comfort her with a lie. *Always a lie.*

She blinked her pale, barely blue eyes, removed the dark wig and pulled the thin turtleneck away. She freed her aching breasts from the tube of rubber that had imprisoned them.

There was no time to think of the past. She had to move quickly, precisely.

She set the makeup kit next to the sink, and began her work.

A few minutes later, an old woman tried the door to the ladies room and found it locked. She raised her hand to knock just as the door opened.

A stunning young woman with porcelain skin, silky black hair and ruby lips brushed past her toward the lobby.

"It's all yours," the beautiful girl said.

Chapter 5

Los Angeles

To Sara, James Cross had always looked more like a *customer* than a coworker - not exactly a compliment when you're a medical examiner.

A couple inches taller than Sara, but reed-thin, pale and painfully soft-spoken; if the guy ever took a nap on his break he'd likely be autopsied.

As he silently sipped coffee alone in the break room, Sara poured herself a cup and sat across from him.

He barely acknowledged her presence. She was used to that with James.

"You get that headless floater this weekend?"

His unblinking eyes met hers.

"Which one?"

Until one corner of his mouth turned up, she wasn't sure that was a joke.

"The one with the hard on."

"Oh...that one. Yes."

He took another sip, his eyes went over her shoulder to the clock on the wall behind her.

"Thoughts?" she said.

"Well. He was very interesting. The stab wounds to the chest would have been fatal, but they didn't kill him."

She nodded.

"Death from decapitation?"

"Yes. You know I'm not on the clock."

She fought the urge to strangle him. She glanced at the clock. It showed 10:12.

"Meet you inside in three?"

"That works for me," he said, quietly.

A few minutes later, Sara and James stood before the wide wall of the dead, a giant filing cabinet of sorts, where the recently autopsied awaited final disposition.

"You sure you want to open this drawer?" James said, "He's a stinker."

Death almost always carried with it an unpleasant, and to Sara, an unmistakable scent, but not all bodies stank. The level of decomposition, circumstances of death, and even physiology, played into it, and the stench of some could be staggering. The cruel "stinker" moniker was given to the worst. Floaters, due to the wet, bacteria-rich environments where they were found, were the worst of the worst.

Sara had already daubed her nostrils with peppermint oil.

She nodded.

Despite that bit of preparation, just opening the door brought tears to her eyes. Once they'd unzipped the bag containing the awful, stump of a figure, now further disfigured by the "Y" shaped autopsy incision from collarbone to pubis, it took all of Sara's training to keep a clear head – and this stinker wasn't nearly as bad as she'd expected.

She looked from James' report to the body, checking the remarks and diagrams against what she saw.

The man's penis, still intact, was at least, finally more or less at rest.

"I made a cast of that for posterity before it dropped. Check toxicology."

Sara flipped to it.

"Extreme levels of theophylline, theobromine, cyclic guanosine mono-phosphate, D-lysergic acid, vaso-dilators, PDE5 inhibitors... and midomafetamine. That'd do it."

James nodded, "Quite a cocktail. Excuse the pun."

She did, though even she had to admit, it was a good one.

"Death by psychedelic aphrodisiac."

"Whoever gave him all that could have saved themselves the knife-work – he was headed for a massive heart attack."

"Still no ID?"

"Narrowing that down with Missing Persons. I expect we'll have that today."

"What about these marks?"

Sara indicated serrations in the flesh at the end of the wrists. A series of semi-circular gouges. With the generally poor condition of the corpse, they weren't obvious, but they were there – a repeating pattern.

"Posthumous. He was fish food for a while."

"Your Time of the Death is Thursday evening to Friday morning?"

"Yes."

"He wasn't in the water very long."

"Long enough for marine life to find him," James said stiffly.

"Did you get photos of these?"

"Not...really pertinent to cause of death."

"But they could relate to the *circumstances* of death -"

"He was clearly stabbed and decapitated."

"Am I interrupting something?" Detective Rick Cromwell managed a smile, even as he backed away from the stench. Neither of them had known he was there.

"How can I help you, Detective?" James asked.

Cromwell ignored him.

"Sara, could we talk for a minute?"

"Sure, what do you need?"

"Concerns the man you're examining. But...maybe out in the hall."

"I'm due for a deposition," Cromwell said as they walked. "I'd like to run some things by you about our floater back there."

"He's not my customer."

It was interesting, Sara mused, how the man could smile and frown at the same time. It was probably endearing to some women.

"But you're interested in the case, obviously."

"Professionally."

He lifted his chin.

Sara wasn't even sure why she'd put it that way.

"Well...they're always a puzzle," she said, finally. "This one maybe more than most."

"Could I get some time with you later?"

"Certainly."

"You have plans tonight?"

"Are you asking me out, Detective?"

The look he gave her was a cross of amusement and genuine surprise.

"Yes. I'm asking you out." His smile was broad this time. "Shanty's? Hermosa Beach – just off the Pier. 7:00?"

She was flabbergasted.

What the hell is wrong with men?

"Shanty's at 7 O'clock." she repeated.

-=-.-=-.-=-.-=-

Shanty's Fish Shack looked like it had risen from the washed-up debris of several wrecked fishing schooners. Whether that was the case or not, Sara didn't know. Despite its proximity to home, it was not one of Sara's hangouts. With its walls draped with old fishing nets and floats, the crusty wooden captain's wheel and rusted anchor chain behind the bar, it attracted equally old, crusty and rusty sailors and long-past-their-prime surfers.

By the time Sara arrived at 7:00 PM, Detective Cromwell, who looked every bit as out of place in his jacket and tie as she felt in her skirt and pumps, already had his big-knuckled hand wrapped around an empty glass.

She'd noticed his hands before. Thick-boned, calloused, a boxer's hands, hardened by countless blows. She knew that look well.

"Sara. Thanks for coming."

"Of course."

She was a little surprised, but realized she probably shouldn't have been when he stood and moved the chair for her. Despite the battle scar on his chin, his overall rugged exterior, he had always been nothing but a gentleman with her.

"I just moved over to this side of town," he said. "Thought I'd check this place out. Know what's good here?"

She looked around.

"My guess would be cod."

He grinned.

"Not exactly your style, huh?"

"Well, no, but it's good to try new things...sometimes."

"Yeah, well...hopefully, we won't regret this." He took a quick glance at the menu. "Would you like a drink?"

She was about to say, "no" when she surprised herself.

"Sure –"

He signaled a craggy waitress with his empty glass.

"Another one of these – and..."

"A Manhattan," Sara said.

"Need some time?" The waitress asked, dryly.

"I'll have the fish and chips," Cromwell said, quickly.

"The same," Sara said.

"Got it."

"Alright," Cromwell sat back. "That's over. So how long have you lived here?"

"In Hermosa Beach, three years...just after USC. Studio City before that."

"California girl all the way."

"I don't surf, but yeah. You're from New York, right?"

"Yonkers."

He laughed when she lifted her chin.

"Yeah, yeah I know. Not exactly Manhattan."

"So, I'll ask the question. What brought you out here?"

"Yonkers."

Now *she* laughed.

The drinks came and even before she sipped, it occurred to her that maybe for the first time since she'd left Deanne back in Arizona, that she was feeling relaxed and at home.

The fish and chips, likely prepared long before Detective Cromwell had arrived, followed quickly behind her first drink. They weren't so bad, in fact, they were pretty good. By the time her second drink came, they'd pretty much finished all but a few fries. Cromwell rubbed the scar on his chin.

"So...now that the food's pretty much gone, are you ready for the second reason I asked you out."

"Our floater."

He nodded. "I didn't want to spoil...this wonderful dinner."

"It was surprisingly good, but no problem – I'm used to shop talk."

"Okay, let's get down to it. I know you didn't perform the autopsy, but from what you've seen so far, what do you think?"

"Well...the cause of death is no surprise – someone cut off his head."

"Got that much."

"The stab wounds through the chest cavity and lungs would have been fatal. His hands and feet were likely removed posthumously to make him tougher to identify. You know there've been a few cases like this – bodies showing up with the easily identifiable features gone. Most were "hits," mob or drug-related, or both. I don't think this was a hit, although it could have been."

"What makes you think it wasn't?"

"Toxicology for one thing. The other is that *hits* seem to go one way or another; either quick, simply to silence the victim, or painfully slow – burns, breaks, gouges, torture; brutality that sends a message.

"Outside of some marks on his wrists I still need to classify, the only real damage done to this guy before his death were the blows that killed him. Torture didn't seem to play into it; based on the type and amount of drugs in his system, making him feel good was just as important as killing him."

Cromwell shook his head.

"Feel good? Oh, yeah...that. But that...uh, happens sometimes when a guy knows he's gonna die doesn't it?"

"An erection? Yes. It can – but it doesn't stay that way...well, for hours on end – PDE5s regulate that."

"PD-whatzit?"

The waitress eyed them, she'd caught at least part of their conversation as she arrived with the check. Cromwell paid it before Sara could protest.

"Mind taking a walk?" he asked.

Not a cloud in the sky as they strolled along the beach, carrying their shoes. After one more day on the unforgiving concrete of the Crime Lab, the cool sand beneath Sara's feet was a welcome relief.

The smog and lights of LA made the Milky Way murky if not completely obscured, but from Hermosa Beach the stars over the smooth water beyond the breakers were bright in the sky, and even the lights of Avalon on the Catalina Islands were visible.

"So...the vazo -"

"Vasodilators."

"Yeah – those, and the PD-whatevers. What are they?"

"Do you ask all the girls about erections?"

He coughed.

"Okay, here's how they work -"

"That much, I know," he affirmed.

"Well, the chemistry is actually interesting."

"You're something else."

"Well...yes. I am."

"Maybe we should just talk about the drugs."

"Okay – I haven't seen the entire report, but along with alcohol, I saw high doses of caffeine, theophylline, and theobromine, they act as PDE-5 inhibitors and vasodilators – they send blood directly to the corpus cavernosum – think of that as the "bone" of the boner, so to speak. In the usual process, another chemical, cyclic guanosine monophosphate, builds up and keeps it rigid – for a while. Normally an enzyme, PDE-5, phosphodiesterase type 5, regulates that process, eventually breaking down the monophosphate. But a high enough dose of inhibitors – and again we're talking massive doses here – would prevent that breakdown from happening."

"So once the flag's raised, it never comes down."

"Exactly. Added to that mix is something that's been around for a while but it's fairly new to the streets – methyl midomafetamine."

"I've heard of that. *Molly*. An aphrodisiac."

"Yes. Molly – some people call it *Ecstasy*."

"So you think this was a sex crime?"

"Has elements of one."

"That explains his...condition...at the end."

"He died happy, certainly. Not exactly the normal ending for a hit."

"But those drugs also could have been used to drop his defenses, right? Get him woozy enough he doesn't see the hit coming."

Sara shook her head.

"That particular mix and dosage would have been a bad choice. Outside of the alcohol, they're not depressants, they're uppers. They'd make him hypersensitive, even schizophrenic, completely out of control. Whoever did this wanted him active – sexually aggressive."

"You learn something new every day," Cromwell mused. "So how did all that stuff get into him – ingested or injected?"

"That's another reason I think this was a sex crime. From the contents of his stomach and liver tissue, I'd say Manhattans and corn nuts were his last meal – he was likely picked up in a bar and injected. I didn't see needle marks in the report, but the missing parts of him would have been obvious entry points."

"Some damn good detective work, Miss Poole. Ever think of getting out of that lab? Over to my side of the family?"

"Hah!"

"I'm serious. You're getting a reputation outside where the air is fresh." "And the men are men?"

"And they aren't in the crime lab?"

"Touché. But at least that's the devil I know."

Purely by habit, she'd started them walking in the direction of her house on the Strand, and now she found herself at her gate.

"Well, this is me."

He nodded.

The night which, Sara had to admit, had been much more comfortable than she'd allowed herself to imagine it would be, even fun, became more than a little awkward.

"Was that the other reason you asked me out? To ask me if I wanted to be a detective?"

An ever-so-slight deepening of those permanent creases in his forehead told her that wasn't the case at all. At least it hadn't been before now.

"Yeah," he said at last. "Anything more I should know?"

Something fell noiselessly but heavily inside her.

"Guarana." She said, finally, "It's a tropical plant. The leaves have high concentrations of some chemicals we found in the victim."

"Tropical? As in Central and South America?"

Sara nodded, "Brazil, parts of Mexico, Cuba – you name it."

Detective Cromwell straightened.

"Which means we still might have a connection to drug gangs and the Mob."

She nodded.

"Good work again," he smiled. "Let me know as soon as you find anything else."

"I will," she said as she watched him go.

-=-=-=-=-

Deanne sipped coffee as she cranked the wheel of the mammoth fiche reader. Working freelance, but back in good graces with the Arizona Tribune, she was happy to take advantage of their archives and news wire. Gray and black flashes of images and print whizzed by, taking notes on a pad sitting precariously over the small space the desk afforded.

She'd searched first for national and then international crime stories, jotting a quick description of cold case and ongoing murder investigations, placing a check mark over any involving stabbings and dismemberment, another on anything with possible drug or mob connections.

And just when she realized she'd spent way too much time chasing stories a long way from home and way too little time on the local news it was her job to investigate, a brand new story came off the wire from New York.

Marco DeMalo, Don of one of the more infamous Mafia families had been stabbed to death during morning rush hour.

It wasn't a dismemberment, wasn't some unidentifiable body dropped in a remote area for disposal. Just the opposite; the sheer audacity of an attack like that on a high-level family member likely took it out of the realm of the crimes she and Sara were looking for.

And yet the story earned two check marks. Mob and stabbing.

She noted New York's finest were looking for a thin, dark young man with little else to go on. Now she had an image, however vague, to place with the crimes.

The DeMalo family, Deanne surmised, would certainly be doing their own investigation…*How does someone have the cajones to think they could ever get away with an attack so bold against a target like that?*

A thin, dark man, apparently. A thin, dark man with a pair of very, very big balls.

Chapter 6
The Mantis

Berlin, Germany
April 24, 1945

Gorain Armanovich Evanov had shot the boy without so much as a thought, his mind as numb and lifeless as the arms that held the heavy Mosin Nagant rifle to his shoulder.

Eyes tearing from the smoke of burning petrol, waste and flesh, he clicked off window after shattered window as he and his brothers crouched, hid, and inched their way forward, shooting whatever moved.

Russian artillery and merciless allied air bombardments had reduced many of the structures to rubble. Most of the remaining windows were shuttered, boarded over or barricaded with anything that could be torn from a wall and nailed or wedged upright. The rest resembled screaming mouths with only a few broken teeth remaining.

Most of these smoking holes were vacant, or littered with human remains – but others held those insane enough to believe their homes, their lives, were still worth defending.

Gorain stepped over the ruined boy. The boy wore an SS jacket meant for a man twice his size. Like so many of the ill-equipped but deadly children defending the shattered streets, he'd been given a salvaged promotion from Hitler's youth to whatever uniform could be stripped from the dead; there were many to choose from.

Bullets whined past his ear and Gorain dropped behind a pile of bricks; his knee cracked against a block, sending white-hot pain through him. A comrade screamed over the thump, thump, thump of machine gun fire.

The young, blonde woman stepped out into the open, shrieking, her face covered with soot, she didn't stop firing until a single rifle-shot threw her backwards onto a pile of bricks.

She crawled, bleeding, back to the machine gun.

The men were on her, howling like savages before Gorain found his feet. They had ripped the bloody clothing from her body, thrown her across the steps of a ruined porch, and begun the rape that would finish the bullet's work before Gorain could test his leg and limp forward.

Horror upon horror.

He understood the men, the brutality, the need for revenge, for the spoils. But now it only added to the sickness in his heart.

He passed the travesty, his eyes, the sites of the rifle that had become part of him now, checking off each window, each darkened space as he crouched, feeling every bit of the pain in his bleeding knee.

Gorain whipped the rifle around the corner from which the blonde woman had appeared.

On this street, several lampposts remained upright.

From each hung the decomposing body of a woman, a boy, or an old man – the strange, terrible fruit of the NAZI resistance. What were their crimes? Too scared to fight? Too old to fight? Had they been suspected or accused as spies, as communists?

Gorain shrank back – a German officer sat at the edge of deep pit in the bomb cratered street, a Luger pointed at his own temple.

Footsteps echoed behind him. Gorain shouted his comrades back, keeping his rifle sited on the officer's chest.

He could see the man take a breath; he gave a resigned smile and blew half of his own face onto the rubble beside him. The officer's body dropped back into the pit.

Gorain and his comrades moved slowly forward. In his periphery, he saw them, regarding, slack-jawed, the bodies of the executed Germans as they passed.

The officer's body lay spread-eagle over a series of steps leading to a heavy steel door.

Gorain and his comrades looked from each other to the body and to the door.

Despite the little information given to foot soldiers by the Soviet command, rumors had spread that Hitler and what remained of his staff had sheltered far beneath the Reichstag.

Where they stood now was far from the Reichstag – but the network of tunnels could be extensive. Could the bomb blast have revealed an entrance? Of course it had, the officer, his one remaining eye staring at the door was a guard!

"We need an officer."

"Have you seen an officer today, Gorain?"

"Hitler's behind that door! We can be the ones to kill Hitler! To finish this!"

They grinned, savagely.

"We'll need explosives to get through that."

"Have you tried the door, Gorain Armonovich Evanov?"

He smiled as they rushed over the body and down the steps. The handle was a pull-down, like a safe. Gorain shouldered his rifle and grasped the handle.

"It's likely booby-trapped," he said.

"After what we've been through. Who cares?"

"Cover me."

The handle clicked, the thick door opened. He slowly moved it wider to the hum and flicker of battery operated lights.

The desiccated bodies of five German soldiers sat in chairs surrounding a small, red box in the center of the room. An open door led to a toilet and a sink. The rest of the room was nothing but a concrete box itself.

"What the hell is it?" Petrov shook his head.

The small box had a handle, but no apparent locks.

"Look at these men. Don't touch it."

"What have we got to lose?"

"Nothing." Gorain said.

He opened the box.

-=-.-=-.-=-.-=-

White. Everywhere Gorain looked; nothing but white. Had he died?

Little by little, the fog began to dissipate. Two gray shadows in the distance. Two men.

"Petrov?"

One of the shadowy figures approached him.

"Petrov is dead. All of the others are dead. Everyone who followed you in, everyone on the street that day. All dead."

Gorain took that in, he, Petrov and the others — none of them expected to live through the final assault on Berlin, and yet, his friend, those men... He remembered the woman and the machine gun, the crypt, and the mummified soldiers surrounding the red box...

The man's dark eyes regarded him. He had thick eyebrows, a long, goatish beard speckled with gray, and a hawkish nose.

Gorain saw now that he was in a hospital room, gauzy, transparent curtains hung all around.

"What was in that box?"

"The final fruit of a German experiment. What do you know about radiation? Atomic energy?"

"Nothing."

The man smiled.

"I'm Igor Vaselyevich Kurchatov. Like you, I live to serve the Soviet. I serve in matters of atomic science. No one who came near that box should be alive today."

"I...opened it. It's my fault."

"You saw those German soldiers. Your comrades, all within several blocks of that box were as good as dead the moment you entered the crypt."

"But I'm alive. Why? I feel strong. I feel fine."

"Strong yes...but fine?" He shook his head. "Time will tell. You survived. Something in your particular genetic structure made you resistant. You've been here ever since."

"I don't know what you mean. I don't understand any of this. I need to go back and serve."

"You have served the Soviet very well here in Arzamas."

"Arzamas? I was in Berlin...yesterday."

"You were in Berlin six months ago."

"Six months. How is that even possible?"

"It's time to tell him, Igor."

40

The other man came forward through the haze. He was thin and young, not much older than Gorain, yet his face was thick-boned, skull-like. Though he wore civilian clothing his deep-set eyes had the frightening fire of blind ambition, the same as the crazed young captains who had ordered so many of his ill-equipped comrades forward into the meat-grinder of German machine gun nests, and death, at Leningrad.

"The Germans surrendered a month after we reached Berlin," he said. "Five months later, the Americans ended the Japanese war – using the power of the atom, the same power you found in Berlin, the power Doctor Kurchatov knows so well."

"The Americans may have ended that war, but they've thrown the world out of balance in doing so," Kurchatov said.

The skull's humorless eyes burned into him.

"You have new orders, Gorain Armanovich Evanov."

"Those soldiers...were dry as mummies. My comrades... If America has the power to do that, what can I possibly do? What can anyone do?"

"For now, you will be assigned to the People's Commissariat for State Security. And you will study."

"Atomic energy?"

"Language and agriculture for now. Your...immunity...could make you valuable on the New Front."

Gorain shook his head.

"What Front is that?"

"The Cuban Front."

Havana, Cuba
August, 1959

The Hotel was between shows and the three men sitting beside the stage talked business the way most men talked baseball; loudly, with an air of care-free belligerence. They spoke in English and if not for the flecks of Italian and Yiddish slang, it sounded much like the conversations Gorain heard daily between any number of American tourists in Havana.

41

Gorain had come to know two of the men very well; the sharp-eyed, diminutive casino owner, Meyer Lanksy and Meyer's rough, broad-skulled friend and associate, Charles "Lucky" Luciano. An exporter of raw sugar and rum, Gorain had developed a lucrative partnership with the two. It was the third man he was here to meet. A virtual block of Sicilian muscle, even as he sat between them, his thick black hair neatly parted and slicked over a head that seemed to rest directly atop his massive shoulders, the man dwarfed the other two — and Lucky, at least, was not a small man.

The conversation barely broke a beat as Lucky smiled his broad crooked smile and waved Gorain over. He rose and bear-hugged Gorain, as he always did.

"This guy!" Lucky said. "Toro – you ever on the lamb, you want to live in style in Cuba – you call this guy."

Meyer, always business, smiled, but remained seated.

Meyer said, "My best friend in the rum trade, Gorain Evanov, meet a true rising star in our business, Toro Borrono."

"A Russky?" Toro said, genuinely surprised, as his huge mitt of a hand shook Gorain's.

"Man does not live by Vodka alone," Gorain spoke in Sicilian-colored Italian.

Toro's eyes went wide, he laughed.

"Oh he's good," Meyer said, "but just try to teach him Yiddish. Oy."

"You need to come for dinner more often, Meyer." Gorain said as he took a seat across from Meyer.

"And how is that beautiful wife of yours?"

"A little under the weather tonight, but Zasha sends her regards."

"Sorry to hear. And Alena?"

"She's...much better."

"Gorgeous little girl," Lucky said to Toro. He looked like he wanted to say more, but Meyer, thankfully, cut that off.

"Toro. Gorain has been very accommodating in moving our product to Florida along with his. Our desire is that as you continue to expand your influence, certain markets in the New York area might open for all of us."

The big man nodded gravely.

"You've built a paradise no doubt about that. All of this we know."

Toro spoke with a quiet eloquence Gorain, frankly, wouldn't have expected given the man's brutish appearance. Lansky had referred to Toro as a "rising star." Now Gorain understood; underestimating this man would be fatal.

"But...frankly, Meyer, we're hearing disturbing things up north. People are talking maybe there's a shift in the wind down here."

"In Cuba the wind blows the way we pay it to blow." Meyer said. "El Presidente Batista can't afford to let it blow any other way. You've seen the uniforms; the soldiers are ours and they're everywhere."

Borrono shrugged.

"What about this Castro?"

"A mad dog," Lucky scoffed. "He's up in the mountains with his tail between his legs."

"It's a dozen guys with old pistols and no bullets, Toro." Meyer assured him.

"We hear the Cubans like him. Russky, you've got Cubans out there in your fields. What do they say?"

"They say what you do," Gorain said. "They're hard workers. They don't have time for a revolution. Castro hates Batista, he loves Cuba. Sugarcane and tourism keep this island afloat and he knows it. If Castro gets in, we pay him like we pay Batista and life goes on."

"See," Lucky said. "This is why I love this guy." He put a broken-knuckled finger to his temple. "Brains."

-=-=-=-=-

"Is there a problem, soldier?"

The soldier gripped his Kalashnikov rifle with both hands as he walked toward her truck from the annato and palms beside the road.

"What are you carrying?"

Zasha Evanova frowned down at him from the high cab. The checkpoint hadn't been here before, that it had been hastily set up was obvious. There were only two others with him. One had stepped in front of the barricade to stop them. He also carried a Kalashnikov rifle. One more guard armed with a .45 caliber pistol, still holstered, stood beside it. Zasha calculated that man's distance from her as 3.2 meters.

She glanced toward the young man in the seat beside her. Rafael's eyes were wide. She turned back to the soldier.

"Farming equipment. Parts for a cane harvester; a combine."

"Ah," he said. "Step out of the truck, please."

"This cargo was cleared at the port."

The soldier cocked his chin toward the Sierra Maestra mountains behind him up the narrow, muddy road.

"You're a long way from the port now, Senora. I need both of you to step out of the truck, please," he repeated.

She nodded to Rafael. He swallowed hard. She turned, smiling, back to the soldier.

"That's fine, check it if you need to," she said as she opened the door. "But we're running behind, is there anything I can do to speed this up?" She put her hand out for his help as she stepped onto the running board. The soldier lowered his rifle as one hand went reflexively to hers.

That was all Zasha needed.

She pulled him toward her and slit his throat. That same knife wickered through the air; the soldier with the pistol was dead before his gun left its holster.

Three rapid shots from Rafael left the last soldier folded over the barricade. Moments later a spray of machine gun fire from the mangroves riddled the soldier's body. He and the splintered barricade collapsed to the ground.

The soldier who had spoken to her, still stood beside the truck, gasping, blood gushing between the fingers he clasped tightly to his throat.

A group of bearded men in tattered fatigues emerged from the jungle, pulling wagons with horses and mules.

Zasha drew a pistol from the waistband of her pants and shot the dying man through the forehead.

The rag-tag soldiers maneuvered their wagons behind the truck.

"A minute earlier would have been helpful," she said to their leader.

He simply smiled, "Kalishnikovs?"

"Counting the two on the ground, two hundred-twenty-six. Six mortars, 200 shells, 200 grenades, and 5000 rounds of 7.62 for the Kalishnikovas. Compliments of Mother Russia."

He nodded.

"Thanks to you and the Mother. Viva la revolución!"

"Indeed. Three of those boxes – the ones marked with black X's – tell your men those stay in the truck. They actually do contain harvesting equipment."

-=-=-=-=-

His name was Jorge and Alena didn't know him any better than any boy at school.

She knew Jorge's face was symmetrical, his dark eyes were aligned well and sat the perfect distance, an eye-width, apart. The split of his wide lips lay at the bisection of his chin and the tip of his nose.   His   ears were perfect mirror images of each other, the lobes projected equally outward. His head was exactly one sixth of his entire height. The fingers of each hand, exactly as they should be. The curves of his shoulders sloped gently, evenly.

She had been told her way of seeing people was odd. She didn't have to be told. Her way of seeing things was only one small piece of the oddness that was Alena.

Among other physical disciplines, her mother had insisted she be proficient in ballet. Their house, which was so much grander than the houses and apartments she daily passed on her way to school, had its own studio complete with bar and wall length mirror. She didn't have to be told she was "odd." The studio mirror told her she was like no one else. In her world of symmetrically different children with their beautiful variations of dark hair and skin, she was hairless and colorless, whiter than white.

But that mirror also told her she too, was proportionally perfect. Perfectly balanced. Symmetrical.

In an odd way, she and Jorge were a perfect match.

And maybe that's why, Alena, who tended to feel little toward the children who either tried to torment or completely ignore her, felt bothered now. Possibly, even, angry.

The class was mathematics but while their teacher, Mr. Robles, noisily scraped problems and possible answers on the black chalkboard at the front of the room, Damasia Abrantes was giving a crude anatomy lesson

45

at the back of the class, raising her skirt a little higher now, spreading her legs a little wider as she slouched lower in her desk, smiling and winking at the nearby boys.

Alena knew it was Jorge's attention Damasia really wanted and she was getting it. As physically perfect as Jorge was, he was also a bit of a rogue. And now he was smiling, staring shamelessly at the panties Damasia was framing for him.

One row over, little Chumo Ybero was trying his best not to stare. Damasia looked his way and nearly laughed out loud. She swung her legs his way, and his head quickly turned forward.

Chumo's name meant twin. He'd had one named Cedro, or so Alena had been told. Cedro had died within a month of his birth. Cedro had been the lucky one.

Obscenely fat, barely five heads high and anything but symmetrical with a left leg that was fully ten centimeters shorter than his right, and one hand that resembled a baby's, Chumo was, in his way, as odd as Alena.

A wave of giggles made Mr. Robles turn back to the class, but only for a moment.

And now that Damasia had Jorge's full attention, she lifted her chin toward Chumo and lifted her skirt higher. Jorge reached over and tapped Chumo on the shoulder. He grinned and pointed back toward Damasia.

Chumo turned, likely more out of reflex than desire, and saw the full view. His chin practically disappeared into the fat folds of his neck, and the entire class broke into laughter. He turned away shaking and red-faced.

Jorge's eyes met Alena's, and, for just a moment stayed there.

"What is wrong?" Mr. Robles turned quickly toward the class, which went immediately silent. He turned back to the board, checking the figures he'd just drawn, as if a possible mistake might have brought their laughter.

Alena felt heat in her own face, a thin line of sweat where the webbing of her black wig met her bald head. Her hand raised to adjust it, and then stopped.

That look had not been revulsion. What had Jorge seen in her?

At the front of the class, Chumo's head was bent forward, teardrops glistened from his desktop.

Behind Alena, she heard Damasia Abrantes giggle.

Alena turned toward her, expressionless.

46

MANTIS

The giggling stopped.

-=-.-=-.-=-.-=-

Alena watched the creature watch her.

Tall, long and graceful, its bulbous eyes set perfectly apart on its triangular head, the mantis was symmetric and hideously beautiful.

Shaded by sugarcane, and perfectly alone, Alena had removed her dark glasses and wig.

Did the creature see her as kin, she wondered? Long, hairless, pale and solitary, they had much in common.

The mantis was there to feast on the larva of the grey beetles and other pests that attacked the sugar cane. Alena had seen the workers string their odd, brown egg sacs in early spring.

So many of the tiny creatures at first...but as summer went on she had noticed fewer and fewer. Those that remained at summer's end were large, like this one, which she judged to be 12.7 centimeters tall.

She replaced her glasses and wig when she heard someone approaching.

She needn't have bothered. It was only Chumo. His uneven footsteps were like a code. Light-heavy, light heavy.

Annoying.

But who else would it be? Jorge, she wished, of course. As school ended, Jorge had been watching her, she knew. And when she'd seen him on the Maracon he always seemed to have noticed her first. He went out of his way to talk to her. But Jorge could be cruel. She knew that too.

"Alena! Are you there?"

"Yes, I'm here. I found a big one. Be quiet, you'll scare it."

He slowed his pace, his fat head poked between the canes.

"Is it a girl?"

"How the hell would I know that?"

He carried a mayonnaise jar with a smaller mantis imprisoned inside.

"Oh, she is! She is!" He said excitedly.

Chumo squatted clumsily beside her and unscrewed the lid, he turned the jar on its side.

"Just watch," he said.

The unflappable mantis had turned its head. She, if she was a she, had definitely taken interest in the newcomer.

The smaller mantis moved toward her – and then he was on her back.

Their tails touched...and melded.

"Oh my god," she gasped. "Are they..."

"They're doing it!" he practically foamed at the mouth when he said it.

Alena watched, fascinated.

The smaller mantis bent his tail and pushed, bent and pushed again, over and over, developed a rhythm.

It was grotesque, insane...and yet.

The female unfolded her long, sawlike forearms, and grasped the male. Her head turned as if she were about to kiss him.

She bit him. She bit him again.

In a flash, his head was gone.

Alena's mouth gaped open.

So completely caught in the act, the male didn't seem to notice or care. His body kept bending, kept pushing, foam poured out of him, poured into her.

He just kept going –

September, 1959

This field would be in flames tomorrow.

Alena carried a cloth bag filled with bright red buttons. She dropped one button on every third stride, passing smoothly between the lush rows of monstrously tall sugarcane, stepping with practiced confidence over the tangled net of brown leaves, her bare ankles avoiding their sharp edges. As summer stretched on and the low leaves browned, they released their sweetness into the air and Alena breathed that intoxicating aroma in with every breath.

MANTIS

The coming fire was a necessary curve in the cycle of the cane's life, death and...whatever lay beyond death; a process that would rid the fields of their decaying leaves, making the harvest of the cane that much easier.

A ritual cleansing of sorts.

When she reached her special place, she crouched in the shade and shelter of those blade-like leaves and waited for her lover to arrive.

-=-.=-.=-.=-

The wailing was awful.

The cries had come from one dream that ended another. A celebration filled with candy and beautifully wrapped gifts had given way to a trapped animal screaming in pain. Pink-skin crackling and charring in the flame; it was much larger than a dog, it might have been a pig...but daylight had quickly faded that image, obliterating it just as the flames had...

A cool breeze swept the awful sounds into her bedroom along with the rich, sweet smell and smoke of the still smoldering sugar cane fields beyond the manor.

Alena fitted the wig onto her bald head then slipped her sunglasses on. She stepped out onto her balcony.

A small crowd had gathered in the courtyard, most of them workers from their plantation, machetes strapped to their hips. The harvest had begun.

In the middle of that group stood Alena's parents, and the wailing woman they were trying so hard to console.

Jorge's mother.

Alena quietly shut her window and closed her curtains to the day.

-=-.=-.=-.=-

Alena blinked. No longer a child, no longer lying in wait on her father's plantation.

The plane was making its final descent. Beyond her window; rooftops, tall buildings, warehouses, hotels, lay in neat asphalt rows. The city of Los Angeles passed beneath her like one more killing field.

Chapter 7

Summer 1968
Culver City, CA

T he young guard smiled, tipped his hat, and waved the car forward past the gates and onto the studio lot.

"Who the fuck was that?" His partner, a three-hundred-fifty pound bag of cannoli flab and tobacco smoke, snorted from the chair of the shaded booth beside him.

"A platinum bombshell in a Bentley T."

"Hah!" The fat man slapped the kid's backside with his hat. "Good work."

Just past the guard booth, the Bentley's shaded passenger window closed.

Alena removed her dark glasses.

Chumo drove between the massive sound stages, unnoticed by the scores of pretty girls, and even prettier men dressed as cowboys, Indians, armored knights, and showgirls.

By the time Chumo reached their destination, the platinum bombshell in the seat behind him had transformed into a bombshell of another kind.

-=-.=-.=-.=-

He had a thing for Elizabeth Taylor.

Not the Elizabeth Taylor of 1968, the pre-1963 model, before Cleopatra. During that production the woman had gone through changes to say the least. From scene to scene, Chad had watched her shift from pixie to plump to pixie again – and back.

Yes, Chadwick T. Maharis had known her in the early days, but despite his wealth, his power, she'd never given in to him. He'd been spurned.

It didn't matter. He had her anytime he wanted now, carrying out his revenge every which way and exactly the way he wanted her. He liked her young and voluptuous, not matronly.

It didn't matter that he himself had the body of the seventy year old mogul he was; a body shaped by decades of booze and indulgence.

When one more stunning Elizabeth Taylor look-alike walked boldly into his secretary's office, the ringmaster of all things beneath Chad Maharis regarded the woman with little more than a forbearing sigh.

Maharis had a studio to run; deadlines had to be met. Never one to leave an opportunity for gratification untapped himself, he ran a tight ship. And right now, he had a problem.

His problem was cocaine, a drug he himself had never used.

But, at this moment his production was in jeopardy. Gone were the days when your own money was enough to carry the day. Today even he answered to a higher power. Lights, cameras, sets, everything and everyone from stuntmen to key grips were heavily insured. While that might seem like protection from failure, a missed deadline assured failure. Miss a deadline close to release and the plug was pulled.

He wasn't going to let that happen to his baby.

But there was a hitch, his star wasn't on set today, hadn't, in fact, been on set for a month. His star was recovering from a wild, destructive bender.

Not only was his star unavailable, that same star had introduced the crew and his costars, including a minor playing his sister, to the poison.

Maharis knew exactly where he got it. The pusher had a cushy, mostly no-show job at the studio.

The man who provided that job was on the other end of the phone right now.

"It's gone too far, Toro. You have to take care of this!"

"He's an impulsive kid. You know how that is."

"He can't work here. He's got to go. I can't have this on my set."

"I know how you feel. I hear you. I want you to know we appreciate what you've done for him, I appreciate what you've done."

"So how do we solve this?"

"It's being handled as we speak. I want to make this up to you. Please accept the special gift I've sent, and my apologies."

"Your gift?"

"Exactly your type with my thanks and blessings. Buon appetito."

The door opened just as Maharis set the receiver down. She was stunning, and absolutely perfect.

"Compliments of Don Borrono," Alena said.

-=-=-=-=-

Sara pulled her stiff neck slowly from shoulder to shoulder as she entered the examination room. She'd had a particularly rough session with the makiwara last night. Even her Sensei begged her to slow down. For whatever reason, she'd been attacking it more viciously than ever lately.

Ben was already taking measurements of the large gray man on table three.

"Morning. So who's come to visit us today?"

"Chadwick T. Maharis."

"The movie producer? No kidding."

He could have been Sara's grandfather; surely he was someone's.

She couldn't remember her own grandfathers, both had passed when she was quite young, what images she had, came from faded gray photographs, their lives were second-hand accounts.

This man was a very, very wealthy grandfather. Manicured, pedicured, even his wavy, silver hair had been colored and conditioned. Between the obvious bruises and abrasions on his chest and throat from last-ditch revival attempts, there was a long zipper-like scar down his sternum, likely to shunt around some nasty plaque in his heart. The procedure was fairly new – and extremely expensive.

"Bypass surgery. Any bets on what brings him here today?" She asked.

"Five bucks on, 'it was his time to go.'" Ben braced himself from the other side of the table. She grasped the old man's wrist.

They quickly maneuvered him onto his side. Ben checked his back, and shook his head.

"Some natural postmortem lividity. No marks of note – whoa!"

"Except for *that*," Sara said.

Just beneath his left ear, a wide, deeply bruised area, opposing half-moons of semicircular cuts. He'd been bitten and bitten solidly – not violent enough to tear out flesh, but enough to dent it and burst the blood vessels beneath. Whatever blood-thinners he'd taken for his heart condition had spread it outward, painted it like a bullseye.

The indented teeth marks, semi-circular, perfect – too perfect, like the marks she'd seen before near the floater's wrists.

Sara straightened, her own heart was beating fast now.

"Roll him back."

Deep bruising of the penis and the area around it. His penile artery had burst.

"Holy crap!" Ben said. "Gramps went out with a bang."

"He was murdered," she said. "We have a multiple murderer."

"What?"

"We need solid photos of that bite; an impression if we can get one."

"Come on, a film producer? Most likely an unintended victim of the casting couch."

"It's more than that. Do you know if they ID'd the headless floater from last weekend?"

"Oof, I saw that one! Yeah, they did. Can't think of the name right off. He was some advertising guy. But Jesus, that was nothing like this."

"Both were obviously having sex when they died. Both were bitten."

"That other guy was fish food. A lot of things bit him."

"Those bites struck me as odd when I saw them, no fish I know of has a bite radius like that – I'm going to have another look at our floater.

"Let's get our mogul's fluids to the lab. With a little luck we can get toxicology going this morning."

Sara fitted a large syringe with a drawing needle.

"Open his eye."

"Multiple murderer?"

From the other end of the line, Sara heard Detective Cromwell take a deep and loud gulp of coffee.

"I'm certain of it," Sara said.

"Are you sure you didn't just call to say, good morning, Rick. What a wonderful dinner that was, can we do it again soon?"

For a moment, Sara was actually speechless. She was talking murder. She wasn't sure if she should be angry...or what. For the first time Sara could remember, she was actually flustered.

"I'm kidding," he said. "I know it was awful. So how do we connect Mister Stumpy with a movie-mogul's heart attack?"

Now she just felt stupid. A slow, calm breath, and she was back on point.

"I haven't gotten the toxicology reports back on Maharis yet. If those show Ecstasy and the active ingredients in guarana that will clinch it based on other evidence."

"What other evidence?"

"Bite wounds on both victims."

"But wouldn't being in the water -"

"I know, marine animals had a feast on the floater, but I saw specific bite signatures on both victims, like human incisors."

"Like human incisors? But not?"

"The position and the cuts are too perfect – they came from a hard metal tool of some kind made to clamp down like teeth. Could be a hand-held device, like pliers, or a denture of some sort."

"Sara...that is...unusual."

"I should say. I read the report on Mister Maharis. The woman who paid him his last visit. Has she been located?"

"Not yet. Long gone before his secretary checked on him. Apparently a long-standing routine with this guy. Elizabeth Taylor look-alike comes in, secretary locks up and takes a long lunch. Miss Taylor lets herself out when the deed is done."

"Elizabeth Taylor look-alike?"

"Gotta love Hollywood."

"Well...Culver City, anyway. So he did this a lot? It's not the same woman every time?"

"There's sort of a stable, if you can believe that. Actresses who...do that on the side...but if you really think you can tie these together I'll take another look."

"That isn't enough?"

"Sara, between you and me, the guy was a heart-attack waiting to happen. Nobody on this end thinks he was murdered. They're going through the motions. Unless murder is beyond doubt, his family wants it kept quiet."

"You mean the studio does."

"It is what it is."

Heat rose in her throat.

"What about the bite wounds?"

There was silence on the other end. Finally, she heard Rick sigh.

"Rough sex. Let me know when you get the test results."

Sara set down the receiver. Generally not one to take the job personally, she was actually shaking.

The clock read ten-fifteen. She had a long day still ahead of her.

Just then, something Cromwell said early in the conversation came back to her.

"I know it was awful."

Had he meant the dive restaurant or their whole evening together? The food wasn't half-bad.

Why the Hell did she care?

Tonight that makiwara was going to wish it had never made its way into her dojo.

-=-.=-.=-.=-

It was another clear, warm and starry evening as Sara made her way back up the beach to her towel and bag. She didn't often swim at night, but sweaty from another long training session, her shoulders and hands aching, a walk down the Hermosa pier just wasn't enough.

The salt air felt good, the slam of the waves, even better.

Just a few people out tonight as she patted herself dry; couples walked hand in hand along the strand, taking in the distant lights of Avalon that shimmered across a quiet sea. A sight, a time to be shared.

She felt a tug in her heart that was becoming uncomfortably familiar.

She had grown tired of the P. Willows scene. As much as she'd tried to make it her own, she'd come to realize it wasn't really. Lately, nothing seemed to be her own.

The short phone conversation with Rick Cromwell had left her angry and disappointed. Was there something more there, something other than professional frustration? She wondered.

Just before her feet left the comforting sand for the concrete "boardwalk," she turned back to the waves. A deep and calming voice came to her.

"I've got you, Sara."

It made her smile.

It was Tahoma's voice, the mysterious man they called Tommy Red Hawk. He'd said those words the second time he saved her life. She and Deanne had investigated him in Arizona only weeks ago. A multiple murderer, Tahoma, whose name meant, quite literally, "the water's edge," was an enigma, an impossibility. A Navajo bent on revenge, he was a shape-shifting *true creature*, a man who could control water, could actually *be* water.

Are you out there, my friend?

Somewhere, she supposed he was.

Call Deanne.

Yeah, she'd do that. Deanne would still be awake.

-=-=-=-=-

"Glad you called, I tried you an hour ago."

"I took a swim out by the pier."

"Wow. That sounds really nice. It's about 10:15PM and 103 degrees here."

"Still don't know how you live in Phoenix."

"Wait...didn't that...stumpy floater wash up on the same beach?"

"Yeah, not far. A little north, why?"

"Never mind. I mean...you swam out there, at night?"

"Hah. Yeah...some things you just don't think about."

"I guess not. Jesus, you're a better woman than I. I've got something."

"Me too – you shoot first."

"Okay. There was a hit in New York a few days ago. A man stabbed a Mafia boss to death in broad daylight."

"Well, that's two elements – mob and knives. Still a stretch though."

"I thought so too, at first. I did some checking into the victim, Marco DeMalo. He was old school. Liquor, prostitution..."

"Booze and broads."

"Exactly. But here's the deal; in the last few years his cousin, Toro Borrono, has been seen with known drug traffickers from Mexico and Cuba."

"Competing revenue streams. Power shift in the family? You think his *cousin* had him hit?"

"Good possibility."

"And some of Toro's contacts are Cuban?"

"Yes... Why is Cuba interesting?"

"Climate, for one – but I guess they both are, I tend to think of Mexico as dry – but that's only the parts I've been too, and the season. It really is tropical and wet in a lot of places."

"Why does wet make a difference?"

"The floater had near-lethal doses of two chemicals from the leaves of a plant that grows in the tropics, Guarana. You see it in South America mostly, but parts of Mexico and certainly Cuba could grow it naturally."

"Okay. So we have a possible south of the border drug connection. With the mob and knives as the murder weapon, both murders get three check marks on the Mulhenney & Poole Multiple Murder Chart."

"The Mulhenney & Poole Multiple Murder Chart?"

"Oh yeah, I'm charting all of this out."

"Good idea – but I mean the name...shouldn't it be *Poole and Mulhenney?*"

"Doesn't sound right."

"Hah! Maybe not to you." It was the first laugh Sara'd had all day. It felt good.

"Okay, maybe you're right, Mulhenny & Poole. Whatever. Here's where the connection breaks down. I had an accidental death come in today I believe is going to be on your chart as a murder as soon as the toxicology report comes in. If I'm right, it's going to tie back to the floater."

"Okay. So where's the break?"

"Both of mine are sex crimes. Yours is clearly not. Only one of mine involved a knife, but both of my victims had enhanced sexual experiences that ended in death."

"Enhanced sexual experiences?"

"That's where the drugs come in. The chemicals from the Guarana leaves speed up the heart and pump enormous amounts of blood to the erogenous zones. The floater also had high levels of a psychotropic sex drug in him they call Molly or Ecstasy on the streets. Today's victim was a seventy-year-old man. He literally had enough of something in him to make his penis explode, at least internally – and his heart and brain went along for the ride. Massive heart attack, massive stroke."

"Jesus. Give me some of that!"

"Last thing YOU need."

How the hell could they be laughing at this, Sara thought? They were describing brutal murders. And in the course of that, they had just dredged up mutual pain from their own not-so-distant past.

Hell, maybe laughing about it was the best thing to do at this point.

"Anyway..." Sara continued, "no knives used were used on the old man, and if my two really are connected the perp is female – a very pretty one apparently."

"Apparently. At least she looks that way with enough drugs in you."

"No, seriously, pretty. Enough to convincingly impersonate Elizabeth Taylor. We have a witness who saw her visit the old man."

"What a way to go – good for him. That does disconnect the New York hit. The witness reports are sketchy, but all of them describe a man."

"So, scratch that one. And I almost forgot to tell you the real kicker that connects my two – both victims had human-looking bite wounds inflicted prior to death."

"Human-looking?"

"The teeth weren't real. Too perfect."

"Well..." Deanne mused, "We've investigated a Navajo shape-shifter made of water, why not a female vampire with dentures?"

Mandeville Canyon

She rinsed her hands twice in the cool water, patted them dry with a fresh towel, and applied alcohol.

The pretty face in the mirror wasn't her own, but it had served its purpose so far.

Alena set her bag on the marble sink. She blinked as she gazed out the wide window and into the deep forest beyond.

In the city, a wide window out was a wide window in, but here in the canyon, shaded from the clear blue skies and bright Southern California sun, her only neighbors would be sparrows, squirrels and the occasional opossum.

She could just see the roof of the guest house from here. That would be Chumo's quarters.

"I'll just be a minute," she said to the door.

"By all means," answered the woman from the other side, "take your time, sweetie. Enjoy that view."

"It is very, very nice."

Alena withdrew one of the small half-moon cases from her bag, pried it silently open as she produced two small capsules from her sleeve, loading one into each of the hollow chambers of the porcelain denture with practiced and calm precision.

It was overkill, of course. But overkill was *certain* kill.

Mother had taught her that.

With her thumb and index finger she pressed the tiny buttons on either side of her palate, releasing, and then replacing her everyday denture with its loaded, deadly counterpart.

She clenched her teeth, felt the familiar, reassuring snap as they set. It always stung, just a little. But pain was the truest sign of life. When her lovers felt no pain, her job was done.

A drop of mint extract from a small vial on her tongue and Alena shouldered her bag. She smiled as she opened the door.

59

The real estate agent was an attractive, if plump, forty-something woman. The woman clicked a switch on the wall and, with a buzz and continuous squeak, the blinds raised to reveal an even broader view of the canyon beyond.

At this time of day, even with the trees, the sun was more evident from this side of the house. Alena blinked at the bright light.

"It's the latest modern thing. You can open and close the shutters with a switch."

Alena replaced her sunglasses.

"Mmm. Very modern. And the view is very, very nice. Still...I'm not sure."

Alena flipped the switch, and the blinds began to squeak closed.

Alena had recognized the woman's weakness on their first meeting. Her willingness to please was more than a sales tool for real estate, it was desperation, both professional and personal. Alena's research had been meticulous. Her name was Audrey Simpson. She was divorced and childless. Her ex had been cheating for years, and immediately remarried. Audrey had no friends, no family. A woman who wouldn't be missed...and knew it.

"But...it's everything you were looking for..."

Alena nodded.

"It's the payment. I'm dealing with a divorce. It's messy. I would need this to be a cash transaction."

"That...can be difficult."

"But not impossible." Alena touched the woman's hand, warmly, the woman swallowed, but didn't recoil.

"No...not impossible..."

"There was only one other buyer, correct? But he's no longer in the market?"

Audrey shook her head, slowly.

"He...seems to have disappeared."

"That's odd, isn't it? We're talking quite a bit of money here - was he a movie star or an advertising executive? Something like that?"

"Advertising. He was...an ad man..."

"Mmm." Alena flipped the switch, the blinds squeaked open, letting the painful light in. She smiled brightly.

"Well, Audrey, his loss can be our gain. How do we make this work?"

Chapter 8

"Cremated? What? They can't —" Sara was incredulous. Heat rose in her throat. She glared at Ben.

"They collected the body yesterday." Palms in the air, he shrugged as if to say, 'It's not my fault, what could I do?' And it wasn't his fault, and there was nothing either of them could do. Sara knew that. Ben was just the closest target.

"The Chief signed off?"

Ben nodded.

"We had evidence!"

"Yeah, pointing to a cerebrovascular accident and myocardial infarction," Ben said.

"But they were sexually and chemically induced!"

"No doubt — but hard to establish foul play." He added, "Especially now."

"What about toxicology?"

"My guess? It's been shelved."

"They can't do this -"

But, of course, they could and had.

"Sara — we looked for a zebra, they found a horse." Ben shook his head.

He was referring to an age-old axiom of forensic pathology — in basic terms it meant the obvious answer is likely the right one. When you see hoof prints, searching for a zebra is a waste of time, the culprit is much more likely a horse.

"Fuck the horse."

"Well...uh. Sara!"

Sara had only just pulled on her gloves - but now she peeled them roughly off. She tossed them toward the bin as she stormed through the swinging examination room door. They dropped to the floor beside it.

"Don't...go out there mad!" She heard him say as the doors swung closed behind her.

She headed straight for the office of the Chief Medical Examiner. Finally, she stopped.

Ben's right.

Not about the certainty of foul play, Maharis was murdered and they both knew it. Ben was right about blowing up on the Chief. She couldn't afford that. Her last foray outside normal channels had brought the Feds down on all of them; she had few enough friends in high places as it was. The ice beneath her was precariously thin.

She shifted gears and took a new direction; toward the toxicology lab.

Unfortunately, it was Merl Boggs manning the desk.

Porky and pink white to the point of chalk, Boggs was more of a mass than a man. His sausage-like fingers tapped the desk in front of him as he glanced up through glasses so thick, his magnified pupils nearly filled the frames. A cup, so old the coffee ring had welded it permanently to the counter, sat beside his tapping right hand.

He cleared a long-hibernating frog from his throat.

"How can I help you, Miss Poole?" He asked.

Tim Reynolds, an intern who no doubt hated life at this point, sat not far from the front desk. He looked desperately up at her from the centrifuge beside him.

She smiled at Tim, and he looked down, sheepishly.

"I'm looking for the report on Chadwick T. Maharis."

"Hmm." Boggs said. Barely turning his body, he flipped slowly through a rolling index not far from the petrified coffee mug.

"I...don't seem to have that. Oh wait. Yes. That has been put on a thirty day hold, pending new evidence."

"The subject's been cremated," she said.

"Then we likely won't be running those tests."

"But the fluids – the swabs, you've kept those?"

"Well yes. Of course. For thirty days."

Sara took a deep breath. All was not lost.

Tim must have felt her staring at him. He looked up at her now. It was obvious he'd heard everything, including the exasperation in her voice.

"If there's anything you can do to finish that report, I would appreciate it very much."

"Well," Boggs said. "As I said, those tests are on hold...and we are very, very busy here."

She smiled past Boggs to Tim.

"Of course you are."

Phoenix, Arizona
Maricopa County Crime Lab

"He's not going to speak to you today," Deputy Fred assured her.

It was one hundred and twelve degrees. Outside of roasting naked in the center of Hell, roasting outside the hospital was the last thing Deanne wanted to do right now.

"We had an appointment."

"He's very busy."

"No he isn't."

"Miss..."

"Deanne. My name is Deanne Mulhenney, Fred. I've been here twice before. You, Deputy Frederick Richard Baker, have been here both times, and you've seen my press credentials. Would you like to see them again?"

The officer sighed. "You know what's going on. He's not seeing anyone...right now."

"No, I don't know what's going on – but Arizonans have a right to know why justice is being delayed, and why a key component of Maricopa County's Criminal Justice system has barricaded himself inside his office."

She pulled her steno pad and a pen from her purse.

"Don't do that, Deanne. I'm not on record."

"Deputy Frederick Richard Baker, how does a Chief Medical Examiner in hiding affect your job as a deputy in the Maricopa Sheriff's Office? Aren't bodies piling up? Shouldn't you be on patrol?"

"I'm not saying anything."

"Why is the Maricopa County Crime Lab using Sheriff's Deputies to shield a Chief Medical Examiner who has been accused of corruption?"

"Don't be a b -" He stopped himself short.

"Could you spell that last word out for me? I only caught the letter 'b'"

"Miss Mulhenney, I'm asking you *politely* to leave."

Deanne stood her ground; still she was surprised when the Deputy stepped suddenly back.

"I have every right to be here," she started, but a large shadow engulfed her before she turned to see her friend, Police Sergeant Bill Henry step beside her. The man was a mountain.

"Afternoon, Fred," Bill said.

"Afternoon Sergeant."

"Deanne, what are you doing out here in the sun?" Bill asked, "They've got really nice air-conditioning in there."

"That's what I hear," she said as Deputy Fred moved to the side.

"Thanks for that," she said to her old friend as they walked together into the narrow lobby. An odd sense of creepy deja vu spread through her; the only other time she'd been inside here, Sara had confidently led the way, "but I could've handled him."

"Sure you could've, Deanne. I'm just here for the coffee." He bent over the big urn that sat next to the reception window, and tapped out a cup. "Like some?"

"You just happened to be driving this way?" She asked.

He winked, and tipped his chin toward the entrance to the lab as one of the assistant Medical Examiners she'd met a few weeks ago with Sara pushed his way through the swinging door, a folder tucked under one arm.

Wavy black hair, pale, but somewhat tall and good-looking without the tape & bobby-pin repaired glasses, she remembered his name was Mark, and he was sweet on Sara.

If he only knew.

"Have a care, Deanne." Bill said quietly. "Touchy situation here. This is not friendly territory right now."

She nodded.

"Tell me about it."

"Call if you need anything," Bill said as he left.

"I will."

"Uh, Deanne," Mark looked furtively toward the glassed-in reception booth. It was empty. "Could you come with me?"

"I'm here to see the Chief -"

"I know. But he's not even here."

"What?"

"There's something else I need to talk to you about."

He opened the door to the little room where she and Sara had viewed grim crime scene photos before, the same sense of claustrophobia and suffocating pall of death she'd felt that day came back as he closed the door behind them.

"I know you've been trying to see the Chief." Mark said. "I called Sergeant Henry when I found out you'd made an appointment to see him today. There's no way they were going to let you in."

"What's going on?"

"I hear it's bad, misappropriation of funds, but I don't know any details and I couldn't tell you if I did." He opened the folder and spread out a slew of gruesome photos across the table.

She took a deep breath as she sank into the uncomfortable chair. The light above was harsh. The change from unbearable heat to the chill and smells of the lab, the awful closeness from this little room…and now these photos.

"Sara called – she wanted me to look for anything like this that came in. She said you'd want to know right away. Would you like some water?"

Deanne nodded.

"I'll get it."

And then Deanne was alone, in what seemed to be an interrogation room, with horrible evidence of violent death.

Another stump case. The body in these photos had suffered much worse decomposition than the one Sara had sent, or any of the photos Bill had given her.

But the wounds were as close to an exact match to Sara's victim as Deanne imagined could be possible. Head, hands and feet were gone. Two wide stab wounds through the rib cage. The victim was male, but, in this case the genitals had been torn off, or had simply rotted away.

No cigar burns or other signs of torture on what remained of the torso – but there could have been, she supposed, decomposition had taken a terrible toll.

She slowly pushed the topmost photos to the side. Underneath, *close-ups of the wrist stumps -*

The door opened behind her.

She slammed back against the chair hard enough to scrape the wooden legs loudly across the floor.

"God!"

"Sorry," Mark said. He set a paper cup of water beside the photos. Deanne downed it like a shot of iced vodka.

She shook her head.

"Thank you, it's not your fault. Are those bite marks on his wrists?"

Mark pulled a chair up beside her.

"Well...they look like bite marks. He was dumped in Sinaloa, Mexico. Obviously the desert took a lot of him before the Federalies found him."

"Do you know who he is...was?"

"It took a bit of work – but we think it's Vincent Romano, a low-level Mafiosa who dropped out of FBI surveillance two weeks ago."

"Mafia? But he was murdered in Mexico?"

Mark nodded. "We think he was making drug connections down there."

"I haven't heard of Romano. What family did he work for?"

"Borrono. What used to be the DeMalo family."

"Used to be?"

"Yeah. There's been a war going on. The business was taken over by Toro Borrono."

-=-=-=-=-

"That's why we have the Associated Press wire."

Gerald Portnoy, who'd run The Arizona Tribune since a little after the invention of ink, looked blandly up from his usual breakfast; onion bagel with cream cheese and a slice of tomato, a cup of coffee and a cigar. The ghosts of breakfasts past lay in crusty remnants between galleys and the faded photo of the family he once supposedly had.

The paper had been in his family forever. It was actually the fourth paper in Arizona, *The Tombstone Epitaph* being the first and the oldest continuously-running paper in the United States, the long-dead *Piñon Rim Clarion*, being the second, and Tucson's *Gazette* being the third.

Gerald was literally born to run this paper, but not to chase down news stories — he'd never actually investigated or written one. His real marriage was to his desk; he rarely left it.

"Gerry, this is big."

"I understand it *could* be. Again, that's why we pay the Associated Press. When I write that check on the 15th of every month I pay their travel, their hotels, their bagels with cream cheese, and they send us their big stories in return."

"A story like this could put the Trib on the map."

He pointed to the map of Arizona tacked to the wall behind him.

"We're already on a map. That one. Where did they find that body?"

"Just south of us."

"Sinaloa, Mexico, wasn't it?"

"*Somewhat* south of us. But it could connect to two murders in Los Angeles — and a Mafia hit in New York."

"Four murders that *could* connect...and none in any city residing in the great, Copper State of Arizona."

"They're connected to drugs that could be coming into Arizona from Mexico — even Cuba."

"Cuba? Now you're even further out."

"Only a little."

"Deanne, I'm going to be blunt. Your coverage of the Worwick Senatorial Campaign was big, that's why you've been given a second chance with the Tribune. But at its heart, that was an Arizona story."

"With national implications."

"But an Arizona story. The Arizona Tribune. See how the word Arizona fits in both of those? We're local."

She nodded, "Yes, I get that."

"Good. You were at the Medical Examiner's office today. Did you get an interview?"

"He wasn't there."

"What?"

"He hasn't been there for two weeks. It's a sham. He's not holed up in the office – he's a complete no-show. The Sheriff's office seems to be shielding him."

"Now that's an Arizona story."

"And I'm writing it."

"Good, have it on my desk by 3 O'clock."

-=-=-=-=-

"So, did you write the story?" Sara asked from her phone far away on the coast of California.

"I wrote *A* story." Deanne, sighed. "It sucked. It needed more. They'll print it, but I'm on borrowed time. Gerry's right. If I want to write for the Tribune, I need to focus on local stories."

A wave crashed loudly from the other end of the phone.

"Is that what you want to do, Deanne?" Sara asked, finally.

Somewhere past the mountain that made up her backyard, there was a full moon. A shudder as remnants of her nightmare came back; once again she looked directly into her mirror with only a full moon staring back, *then a muzzle flash as that mirror shattered.*

Deanne had moved from Margarita to Bourbon on ice. She took another sip as she listened to the waves.

What must that be like, she wondered? Living so close to the beach? *Paradise.*

"You know I don't." That's what she wanted to say. Instead, she said, "I don't know what I want right now. I'm tired of the game. I know the two of us are onto something important – something deadly and frightening on a big scale – and no one who can do anything wants to listen."

"Tell me about it. I'm being stonewalled over here too. They cremated the producer's body."

"What? They destroyed the evidence?"

"It may not be a total loss. The samples I took are still there – at least for a while. I have a friend on the inside."

"Let me guess...a young man?"

"As it turns out..."

Deanne shook her head. She'd kill for the power Sara held over men without even wanting them. Maybe that was Sara's "super power." Not wanting them. Deanne actually chuckled.

"What?"

"Nothing. But the reason I called is your new best friend at the Maricopa County Crime Lab, Mark, found a body that fits."

"Great! I called Mark after the floater. He said he might have something – but it was too early to tell. What did he give you?"

"Another stumpy hit. This one was in Sinaloa, Mexico. Here's the deal, not only was the victim an American making drug connections in Mexico - he'd been under FBI surveillance. He worked for the Mafia boss that was murdered in New York."

"That is big. So your New York City hit is back on the Mulhenney and Poole chart!"

"Yes. With a major new check mark. And the Sinaloa victim has four checkmarks: Mafia, knives, drugs, and, drum roll...there are what appear to be bite marks on his wrists."

"Appear to be? Mark wasn't sure? Does he think the tooth marks are too perfect?"

"Too much decomposition in this case for Mark to say; Romano had been out in the hot sun for quite a while."

"Okay. I've got to get those tests run somehow. It's going to be tough."

"Ruffling feathers?"

"Way beyond that. It may cost my job – my connection's job too."

Deanne finished her drink in a very loud gulp.

"We're both on very thin ice."

"To put it mildly. If we do this, we're going rogue."

Going rogue. Sara wondered how something so potentially destructive to her career could possibly be so familiar...even comfortable?

Sara set the receiver down, listening to the rush of not-so-distant waves. She could easily have suggested Deanne pack her things and join her. But she hadn't done that.

In a very real way, Sara had gone rogue most of her life. It wasn't easy. She wondered if Deanne had the stomach for it.

That isn't for you to say.

The phone rang again. Maybe she'd say something this time.

The cacophony of loud talk and music coming from the other end of the phone took her by surprise.

"Sara?"

"Detective Cromwell?"

"Friends call me Rick sometimes."

"I don't have any test results - they cremated Maharis."

"What? No...I'm not calling about that. About the other night... *Did you say they cremated him?* That was fast."

"You're telling me."

"That's... Wait, can we just start this conversation again?"

"How can I help you, Detective?"

"Are you always on the clock? Don't answer that. Have you had dinner?"

"It's after nine, so yes..." The sad tin from her barely-warmed Mexican-style TV dinner, spattered with paste-like refried beans, still sat on her small Formica table. "I've...eaten. Are you asking me out again?"

"Yes."

"Are you at a bar?"

"Technically. I'm just using their phone. I'm close – I'm in Santa Monica."

"You're on the right coast anyway. If you don't mind heading south there's *Loosies* in Manhattan Beach."

"Is it nicer than Shanty's?"

"You've set a high bar there; fewer pirates anyway, and they even have music."

-=-=-=-=-

"I was looking for a sign that said, *Lucy's* with a 'u,'" Cromwell said as he slid into the booth, stopping a respectful distance short of Sara.

"That was an initiation. I could have told you how it was spelled, but then you wouldn't have passed the test."

He shook his head.

"You're something else."

"So I hear." She signaled a pretty, trim, short-haired waitress in a black turtleneck, "Jack, straight, right?"

"Ah – yeah," Rick said, clearly used to doing the ordering.

"Lucy – Manhattan for me, brand doesn't matter, Jack straight for my friend."

The girl nodded.

Rick said, "that'll work. You come here a lot? You know her?"

"All the girls who work here are named Lucy. It's sort of an in joke.

"I used to come here a lot – I strayed into the city for a while."

From a small stage near the bar, a young woman strummed her guitar softly, singing a slow, smoky version of Simon And Garfunkel's *Mrs. Robinson* under the mote-filled spotlight.

Rick scanned the clientele at the bar. It was an eclectic group, not the typical beach crowd. Gray-haired business suit execs, young trim men in turtlenecks, attractive, well-dressed young women in black, some wore berets, the local Communists.

"Reminds me of the Village," he said. "Greenwich."

Sara smiled.

"I imagine so. Did you go there often?"

He laughed, "No. Not at all."

Lucy served their drinks, the Manhattan was sweet, the warmth spread quickly; it felt good. Sara thought of Deanne, but the scent of Old Spice brought her back to Rick.

"So you were in Santa Monica today?"

"Eh, that's work. Running down a lead. Nothing you wanna hear about. Thinking about maybe moving to this side of town, anyway."

"Rents are cheap."

"That's not a problem where I live either. I'm over by the reservoir."

"Silver Lake?"

"Yeah. Even cockroaches can afford it. More move in every night."

"Hah, yeah. There is *that* downtown. The shelled creatures here tend to be edible. I love having the ocean so close."

"Hard to beat."

"Mmm. Something about water. I've always loved it. I was a diver as a kid."

"You mean like scuba?"

"No. Like backflips and swans."

"Ah, a *diver* diver."

"Yeah. Like that," she laughed. "I used to compete."

"I do a mean belly-flop."

"I'll bet you do."

"I was never that...coordinated. I played some football. Did some boxing. Golden Gloves – but..." he rubbed his scarred chin, "...let's just say I was on the receiving end more than I should have been."

"I know what that's like...I do some martial arts. Karate, jujitsu."

"I had a feeling you did something like that. The way you, you know, the way you carry yourself."

"And how do I carry myself, Rick Cromwell?"

"Straight up. Confident."

She considered that as she ordered another round.

The tide was out as they left Loosies.

"Did you walk here?" He asked.

"You are one hell of a judge of distances," she laughed. "I have walked home from here at night before. Not tonight. It's a hike."

"I'll walk you to your car."

Gallantry isn't free, she thought. It comes with a price.

Sara put that thought aside.

"I didn't mean to come off like a jerk about Maharis this morning," Rick said. "Ending that investigation."

"I thought we weren't going to talk shop."

"No, look. It's...more complicated than that. That's all I want to say."

"What do you mean?"

"Nothing."

"Well, now I'm intrigued."

"Forget I said it."

Parking had been wide open tonight. She could easily have parked on the main street. She hadn't, instead she'd parked next to a wall on a blind side street. Was that on purpose, she wondered? Was it some kind of test – and for who, for Rick or for herself?

"Is this you?" Rick asked.

"Yes. Well, thank you again for-"

He kissed her.

Angry heat poured through her. Her body went rigid.

Rick stepped suddenly back.

"I shouldn't have-" he said.

Weeks ago, she had said exactly that to Deanne.

"Don't," she said, "please, don't say that." Sara pulled him back to her. She kissed him tenderly, but fully on the lips. "Don't ever say that."

Her next kiss wasn't tender at all, it was forceful and fierce. She tasted the heat of him.

Suddenly, she didn't know what to say, what to do.

It was that lightheaded sensation she had felt before. The moment of decision just before that blind backwards fall, the leap of faith toward victory or disaster.

And she saw that in his eyes too.

She thrust her hands beneath his shirt, felt the powerful, bare muscles of his back.

"Do it..." she said, hardly recognizing the guttural voice as her own.

Chapter 9

"Welcome to Mandeville Canyon!"

Chumo stared blankly up at the tall thin man in the blue velvet jacket standing outside his door. The man's hair and thin mustache had been dyed to match his jet-black toupee. He carried a large basket of colorfully wrapped fruit and bread. How he had negotiated the steep path down to their home carrying that basket, wearing silk loafers that were little more than slippers, Chumo had no idea.

Worse yet, the man had simply walked around their gate. There was, as yet, no fence around their property, the steep undergrowth-choked terrain and tree cover that rendered the structures practically invisible from the road had provided enough seclusion and security for the previous owner. That would be remedied.

The man thrust the basket toward Chumo.

"I'm Prentice Perkins," he stated with the practiced humility of someone who expected to be recognized. "Yes, the same." He assured Chumo as if he had been.

Chumo nodded dutifully. He took the basket.

"Charles Darrow."

Prentice seemed to check the bank of celebrities in his head, finding no match he said,

"Yes, of course."

The intrusion was unexpected, to say the least. The agent had assured them this was a discreet community of very, very private people. This was not good. Not good at all. Alena would not be pleased.

A pulse of pain in Chumo's temples as the grand front door of the main house opened, and Alena, resplendent in red silk robe, her makeup meticulously if hurriedly applied stepped out. A curious, but welcoming smile on her beautiful face.

She looked exactly the way movie stars are supposed to when they rise in the morning – perfectly coiffed, perfectly made up, perfectly stunning.

The man's jaw nearly struck his collar bone.

"Good morning, Mrs. D –"

He cut the greeting short. Chumo knew the man was putting two and two together – he had, after all, rung the bell on the service door, not the main one – and Chumo could never be married to this goddess.

"Helena Nichols, call me Helen." She took the basket from Chumo, "how very nice."

"This is our neighbor," Chumo said. "Prentice Perkins."

She nodded as if impressed.

"Well, two doors down, anyway," Prentice chirped, "Harry Champlain is just below you." He lifted his chin slightly southwest, as if the house could be seen from here. It couldn't.

"Helen, I'm so pleased to meet you. I was just about to tell your – Charles here, this property was once owned by Cecil B. DeMille."

"Really?"

"One of his properties anyway. Of course, he had the house in Bel Air.

"I'm sure you've wondered about the tunnels under the house? They lead all the way down to the creek. The main structure was a speakeasy. At least upstairs, it was. *Prohibition*. You know. Big parties and liquor. When the police came knocking – his guests simply disappeared."

"That's quite a story."

Her eyes met Chumo's and returned to the man. It was subtle, a silent message he knew very well. This was a situation that could take *special handling*.

"I hope we'll have some time together soon. I'd love to hear it."

"Oh. Yes. Of course, I'd like that very much. Oh, in fact – I'm having a party this Friday evening. I'd love it if you came."

"Two doors down, Friday evening."

"You've got it. Eight O'Clock, but you can come early, anytime actually."

"Charles. How do we look for Friday?"

"I'll need to check your schedule."

"What shall I bring?"

"Oh nothing – we're well stocked," he laughed. "Hope to see you Friday, then." With a tiny wave of his hand, he turned up the hill to go. Thinking of something, he turned back.

"Actually. You can bring meat if you like. We're vegetarian. I saw that big truck from American Coolers parked here last week, I'm guessing you had a game locker installed. Several homes in the canyon have them. I couldn't kill a fly – but to each their own."

Her glance toward Chumo left no doubt this time.

She said nothing.

"Do you hunt?" He asked.

"Sometimes."

"Well that is something." He smiled brightly, "a beautiful young woman who hunts. Don't let Harry Champlain talk your ear off!"

And with that, the strange man made his way back up the hill.

-=-.=-.=-.=-

Plainfield, New Jersey

The books that lined the shelves of the small library had come with the gated mansion. They wouldn't be read. The prior owner was forced to leave quickly and it would be a miracle if anything but the maid's feather duster disturbed any of them ever again.

Don Toro Borrono filled the walnut desk at the apex of the room. In the ten years following his first meeting with Meyer Lansky in Havana, Borrono had grown in both stature and girth; the leather throne behind that desk barely contained him. Cradled in his bear-like paws, his espresso cup looked comically tiny, as though it could have come from a child's kitchen play set.

But Tony, "The Hammer," Buldoni, the man who stood nervously on the other side of that desk was in no position to see the humor in that.

"Don Borrono, I know why you sent her. I'm happy that...tick is off my back. I appreciate the effort. But, now it's over. No one's in our business."

The newly-minted Don stirred two cubes of raw Cuban sugar into his espresso. He said nothing as they melted away.

"Business is better than ever," Tony went on. "It's aces. So...why is she still in Los Angeles?"

Borrono took a sip. Satisfied the bitterness was gone, his steel-gray eyes locked, finally, on Tony's.

"Sometimes it's good to have one more ace up your sleeve." Toro said, flatly.

"I would have taken care of that problem myself if I thought he'd go anywhere with it."

"And how would you have done that, Tony? Rip his eyes out with a claw-hammer? Crush his knees on the set?"

He was referring to two very public messages Tony had personally delivered early in his career. The sheer brutality of those attacks had made Tony's *bones,* he moved up the ranks because of them. They had also cost him five years in Attica, a fortune to keep that sentence to only five, and had brought a great deal of unwanted attention to the Borrono family.

"With all due respect, that was some time ago."

The Don nodded slowly.

"This was a situation that required a certain amount of finesse. With all due respect, finesse is not a quality you're known for."

"I don't need the Aliena looking over my shoulder."

Don Borrono set his cup abruptly down, his jaw set tight.

"That's why I brought her home last night, Tony. She's waiting in the other room."

Tony's normally olive skin blanched, his eyes went wide.

When the door behind him swung quickly open. Tony nearly leaped out of his alligator shoes.

"Boo!" Johnny Borrono laughed as he sauntered through that door.

Just as tall as his father, Johnny was every bit as imposing, even without the girth. His good looks and smile had come from his mother, so had his notorious hair-trigger temper and ruthlessness.

Don Borrono smiled, then laughed deeply.

"Suddenly, you're respectful."

78

Tony, his forehead shiny with sweat, chuckled uneasily, his laughter, when it came, was every bit as uneasy.

"That was good," he lied. "Okay, okay, that was good."

"Tony," Johnny laid his hand on Tony's shoulder. He gave him a pat that made Tony jump.

"She's ten miles from where you stand? You better hope *that name* never slips out your mouth."

Johnny waited for the door to close behind "The Hammer." He sighed.

"Poppa, I know Tony lets his clients get too close. He forgets it's a business, not a party. Letting that little kid get hooked — that was bad for business. Tony needs guard rails, sure. But he is loyal."

Toro set the ever-present cigar on its tray and folded his arms. His steely, olive-green eyes glinted beneath the thick ridge of graying brow. Johnny knew the look, it meant tread softly.

"Don't tell me something I don't want to hear, Johnny."

Johnny nodded.

"I don't want to give Tony credit for deep thought, which we both know he doesn't deserve, but he's not entirely wrong on this. Did you give Alena the okay to buy a house in Los Angeles?"

"I pay her solid coin. She earns it. She wants a house, she has a house."

"She wasn't the first in line for that property, you know that, Poppa."

Don Borrono sat back and the chair didn't so much squeak as groan with the shift.

Then he raised his hands and laughed.

"You think I was first in line for this place?"

"I know you weren't. I also know you didn't whack the guy who was."

"Seems like you've been doing a lot of looking into your cousin's business."

"You *want* me to do a lot of looking. Don't throw that back on me. Alena, she's like a little sister to me. But, I gotta tell you, Dad. She's freelancing. And that's not good for business either."

-=-=-=-=-

"Helen! Charles! You came! How wonderful!" Alena took the peck on her cheek from Prentice Perkins with practiced good nature.

Chumo uneasily did the same.

The pretty young man who had opened the door for them had quickly melted into the perfumed milieu, and Prentice, dressed in a fire-engine red smoking jacket tonight, ushered them through the entry calling for his roommate, Walter. The mostly aged, but well-kept, expensively-if-slightly-out-of-date-dressed, guests fought to acknowledge the odd pair without gawking.

It was, of course, Alena, dressed in a low-cut body-hugging shell that threw light from every curve of her, who captured the envious eye of every female, and the awe of every male. Chumo, of course, was merely an oddity.

If only they knew, he thought.

"This smells wonderful! Even to me! What's in it?"

"Pork, mostly." Alena smiled.

"Let's get this to the dining room."

They were offered a choice of either champagne or drinks so strong the alcohol cut through the stifling mix of perfumes and colognes in the air.

Chumo declined. He tried not to frown when Alena scooped a glass of champagne from the tray with a motion as natural as breath.

A man, maybe ten years younger than Prentice, dressed in the same style of red smoking jacket, raised his arms.

"I'm Walter – and you must be our new neighbors!   Charles, you are one lucky man! Helen, forgive Prentice, he only described you as beautiful – I swear I could just eat you up!"

"You're too kind," she said, accepting yet another peck on the cheek.

"Walter!" A woman whose face was familiar, at least a much younger version of it, from movies whose titles Chumo couldn't quite place, called out to the man. Walter grudgingly left them.

Prentice handed her casserole to another young man who placed it carefully among the various treats, mostly raw and roasted vegetables, on the long dining room table.

"Before I set you free to mingle," Prentice said, "I have a few introductions I simply have to make. And one in particular..."

He motioned them both to a study dominated by a grizzly bear standing, incongruously, in one corner of the otherwise delicately appointed room.

A small group of attractive females, aged forty through sixty, Chumo assessed, sat forward in plush chairs, thoroughly engaged as a tall, silver-haired man with a broad white mustache held them spellbound. His voice was deep but soft as he spoke, gesturing to the beast behind him.

"*That* was a gift," Prentice sighed. "From Harry of course. I simply couldn't refuse him."

Without breaking stride, the silver-haired man smiled with a knowing appreciation when he saw Alena.

Alena's sigh was ever-so-slight. No one but Chumo could have heard it, or recognized the danger in it.

Chapter 10

I t couldn't have happened.
But it had.

Sara stepped backwards through it now, rewinding.

The stabbing pain. The sheer panic.

Cool water raining down on her.

Sara had done it. Failure after failure and then...the push off of blind faith, the forward tuck as the deadly, unyielding platform sped past so close she could feel it there even as she passed it by, *the spread, then the knife-like point as fingers met water. The explosion of breath, of water, of exhilaration.*

A joy so clean, so pure.

When she broke back through the surface, *he* was there, sharing that moment, that victory with her, and she loved him for it.

Cool water raining down on her.

Sara closed her eyes and let the cool rain fall.

She reached blindly for the towel where she'd always hung it, but her hand felt...only the rail.

She opened her eyes.

Coach Davis held the towel out to her.

"Sara? What? You were -"

Rick Cromwell, bare-chested in Sara's bed, a thick animal vapor surrounded them both. A throbbing between her legs.

"Sara, what's wrong?"

"Get out."

"What?"

"I said, get out. Get out of my bed. Get out of my house."

"Sara, you had a nightmare. I thought -"

"I know what you thought. It isn't going to happen."

He blinked.

"But -"

And then she was running through the darkness, through the house, over her gate and past the other houses. Her feet sank into the dry sand. She kicked her way forward to the firm wet pack and ran on. And when she reached the sea, a roaring wave leaped up to take her.

Sara screamed as she dove straight for its heart, and exploded inside.

"Accidental drowning," Sara said, flatly, removing her gloves.

The blue corpse of a ten-year-old girl, the cruel Y-shaped dissection wound ready for stitching, lay naked on the table.

"That's a wrap," Ben said.

Sara nodded, pulling her soiled whites away as she headed for freedom.

"That was tough," Ben understated.

"Yeah. That was."

She tossed the gloves and whites into their respective barrels and pushed the doors wide.

"Sara?"

Ben had followed right behind her into the hallway.

"What?"

"You wanna get a drink? Go to that Pussy Willow place?"

Despite the deep hole she felt inside, it almost made her laugh.

"It's P. Willows — they don't actually...spell it out."

"Oh, yeah. Okay, I get that."

"You'd actually go there again, wouldn't you?"

"Yeah. If only to watch you beat up college pukes."

"Hah!"

She shook her head.

"You're a good guy, Ben."

"Does that mean, no?"

She sighed.

"I wouldn't be good company tonight."

"You never really are."

"I take that 'good guy' thing back. *Shithead.*"

They both laughed. It felt good.

"Okay. Sure. You really want to go there? We can go anywhere."

"Yeah. It's boss, kind of like having Halloween any night of the year."

"Ah...that's one way to see it. Okay. I've got a couple things to do first and I'll meet you."

"No way I'm going in there alone."

"I hear you there. Meet me outside Canter's Deli. It won't take long."

She walked into the women's washroom, waited a few moments, and then, once Ben had cleared the hallway, she headed the other way, to the Toxicology Lab.

Thankfully, Tim Reynolds was at the front desk. But Merl Boggs was still there she saw his wide backside on a stool in a back corner. He was staring into a stereo-microscope, jotting notes on a pad beside it.

Sara smiled as she handed Tim a manila folder with a list of case numbers scrawled on the front.

He looked quickly back at Boggs. Then he nodded, flipping the index card roller.

"Let me check these."

He disappeared behind a row of cabinets with her envelope in hand. He returned quickly.

"No." He slid the folder across the counter. "None of these cases are due for another 24 hours."

"Okay, just thought I'd check."

Tim bit his lip and tapped the folder where the edge of a typed report protruded. He slid that report all the way inside.

Sara silently mouthed the words, "Thank you."

-=-=-=-=-

In the end, coffee and the comforting aromas wafting from Canter's Deli were a stronger draw than Manhattans in the decadent carnival that was P. Willows.

Nothing like thin-sliced brisket on rye to take your cares away.

Sara wolfed her sandwich down between gulps of strong black coffee as if she hadn't eaten in weeks.

"Wow!" Ben said, still holding the first half of his pastrami in his hand as he watched her finish. "Don't even think you're getting any of this."

She pulled a thick fry off of his plate and practically inhaled it, glaring at him.

He yanked his plate away from her.

It felt good to laugh; to be full, satisfied.

And then, from out of nowhere...tears.

"Hey. I was just kidding. Take the sandwich."

And then she was laughing again.

Their waitress, coffee pot in hand, eyed the empty plate she'd set in front of Sara just moments before. Only the garnish remained.

"What? You didn't like your parsley?"

She refilled their cups and walked away, shaking her head.

That got them laughing again.

"I love this place." Ben said. "I come for the service."

"It is a proud tradition. Surly. You've gotta love it."

Ben took another bite. He washed it down with coffee, chased it with ice-water, and leaned forward.

"I don't think I can do it anymore," he said.

It took Sara aback. Wrapped in her own pain, it was exactly what she'd been thinking, but it was the last thing she expected from Ben.

"Forget I said that...maybe, I just needed to say it. But I know you feel it too...sometimes you don't hide it."

She nodded, not knowing what to say. How could she possibly help him when all she wanted to do was run away right now. Not just from this conversation, from the horrors of their profession, from everything.

"It's..." her voice trailed off, it was as if her tongue had forgotten how to do its job.

"Not for everyone." He finished for her. "I know. I thought it was for me. I joke around while we do it. But...how many drowned kids, murdered kids -"

"We can't think of them that way." It was the right thing to say and still it was a lie; a lie you trained yourself to say, to believe.

He nodded.

"I know. I pretend I don't. I spend all day pretending."

Sara walked Ben to his car in silence, unable to ignore the feeling that this simple, normal deed was an odd, sad parody of last night's disaster.

"See you in the lab tomorrow?" She said, as he pulled out his keys. It wasn't really a question. She knew what his response would be.

"Yeah," he nodded.

Before she turned to leave, she kissed him softly on the forehead.

It caught him by surprise at first, but then he nodded.

"Thank you for that," he said.

As she walked back toward her car, she heard him ask, "you're going there, aren't you?"

"I'm going home." She kept walking.

"Look. I don't understand...any of that." Ben said, "But...at least you have *something*, Sara."

Sara slipped out her keys as she approached her car. She sighed. Finally, she dropped them back in her purse and kept walking.

Moments later, she felt the cool, smooth leather of a booth at P. Willows beneath her thighs.

"Your usual, Traci?"

Sara nodded to the waitress.

The woman arrived shortly after her Manhattan did. She was pretty, full-figured, maybe a few years older than Sara.

"I'm sorry, I couldn't help noticing you walk in. Do you mind?"

"Not at all," Sara said.

The woman sipped her dirty Martini cautiously, holding the glass with both hands, as if someone might whisk it away at any moment.

"I'm only in Los Angeles for one night. I was curious, but this place scares me a little."

Sure you are, and sure it does, Sara thought.

"No need to be scared," Sara said. "Go with your feelings..."

The woman's hand was soft and warm as it slid beneath Sara's skirt, Sara drew in a breath with her touch.

MANTIS

Sara tasted salty olive and expensive vodka in her kiss.

Chapter 11

C humo sipped his coffee as he pretended to skim The Los Angeles Times.

Across the table, perfect Alena lifted one more perfectly carved red cube of raw steak to her lips. She bit down once, then sucked it down in that way she did. She smiled and the crimson between her impossibly white teeth matched the red of her lips.

Her hair was platinum this morning. The wig, the make-up was a habit, Chumo supposed. There was no reason to make herself for him, all of her charms, secrets, and horrors, were as open to him as the blue silk robe draping her shoulders.

"And what is it my Chumo doesn't want to tell me?"

"You're being reckless. You know it. I don't need to tell you."

"Is Chumo jealous?"

"Is Alena an ass?"

They both chuckled.

She'd actually brought him home; their new neighbor. The mustached, big-game hunter. She'd purposely left her window open to Chumo's window. Chumo had seen everything, heard everything...as he had since her very first time.

"What are you going to do with him?"

Instead of pouring her own coffee, she took a sip of his. When she set the cup back on his dish, a bloody red kiss dripped from the rim.

"What I always do. Make him happy...for as long as I want to."

"You bought this house. He's our neighbor."

"Makes it interesting, doesn't it?"

He glared at her.

"You can't walk away from this one."

"I'll take care of it."

"You make the mess. I'm the one who cleans."

"And I love you for that."

"Don't patronize me. I'm not the only one who doesn't like this."

Her painted eyebrows raised, if only slightly. One part of Alena's daily ritual, the choosing and insertion of her colored contacts, had yet to be done. As she gauged the depth of Chumo's concern, the nearly transparent gray surrounding the black hole of her pupils contracted, the cold, reptilian sight of that would likely have frightened most men to death. To Chumo, who saw beauty in every part of her, it simply meant he'd caught her attention.

"Well, Chumo," she said, glancing over his head to the clock behind him. "Our workday begins. Another mess to make, another to clean."

She cinched the robe tight to her trim waist and pressed her lips to his bald pate as a mother would a newborn.

"Uncle Toro loves me. I'll deal with him."

-=-.=-.=-.=-

He was a man who never was completing a mission that never happened. Timing and placement told him almost everything he needed to know.

Other than the time and place, he knew a special package was being held for him in Griffith Park. His mission would be the pickup and on-time delivery of this package to a safe-house near the Ambassador Hotel in Los Angeles.

He knew the mission was critical. If it hadn't been, he wouldn't have been chosen. He had the necessary training, clearances and identification, and he spoke Russian.

Outside of Russian-speaking, he knew the package was female, old and she would be frightened to death because she knew something.

Exactly what she knew, wasn't his job to find out.

He wound his way up the road. When he saw three freshly planted cypress, he turned deep into the park. He shook his head. You didn't need to be a horticulturist to know those trees wouldn't last two weeks in that shade.

After one more fresh cypress, he stopped the car. He checked his watch, waited two minutes, and began the short hike to the package.

A cool morning, but even at that, the woman was overdressed in a hooded coat and black gloves. A scarf covered most of her face. A single lock of gray hair shook over her dark glasses as she trembled, one infirm hand grasped the concrete bench for support.

"Eto prekrasnyy den', mama."

She nodded.

"Da, eto prekrasnyy den'." Yes, it was a beautiful day, she agreed, hoarsely.

It was sad. She was someone's grandmother, likely here illegally. Whatever she knew, whatever the Americans had promised her – the last of her years would be shit.

"Ty milyy." You're sweet, she said, she bent to kiss the hand he offered as she rose.

Instinctively he pulled his hand away, but the sting of her bite was cobra-fast.

She rolled with his kick, taking his leg and her full weight over the bench, his testicles blasted with paralyzing force against its concrete back, as she rolled to her feet in the soft grass behind it.

Before another breath could fill his lungs, Alena's teeth sank deep into his neck.

Moments later, a young, if incongruous, laughing couple, a beautiful young woman and a short fat balding man hugged each other tightly, doubled up on their Vespa as they drove northwest out of Griffith Park toward Burbank.

When they reached Forest Lawn Drive, they loaded the Vespa into a green panel truck and drove to their new home in Mandeville Canyon.

The unmarked helicopter picked up the car it was looking for, the one with the blue circle on its roof, as it broke through the tree cover of Griffith Park, headed south. It careened straight across Los Feliz Boulevard and slammed with crushing force into an oncoming cement truck.

90

The first to the scene confirmed the car contained a man who never was and a package that was broken and no longer useful before they removed the magnetic circle from its roof, and melted into the crowd. The car burst into flames.

-=-=-=-=-

Deanne pressed her fist to her lips, watching the horror flash on the black and white monitor at The Arizona Tribune as the AP wire clacked its updates and the phones rang off the hook.

Only weeks since her coverage of Senatorial Candidate Todd Worwick had ended in murder, the Presidential hopes, and possibly the life of Senator Robert F. Kennedy were ending on the kitchen floor of the Ambassador Hotel.

Several hours earlier, Kennedy had won the California Democratic Primary. The former Attorney General, and the brother of former President John F. Kennedy, whose own life was taken by an assassin's bullet five years before, Senator Kennedy was on his way – that's what tomorrow's headline was set to say. But moments after he'd given his victory speech, shots had rung out.

The primary was why Deanne was still in the office after midnight.

"How does something like this happen?" Collins, the sports editor stood, arms folded, behind his desk, his eyes glued to the television like everybody else.

"Where was the Secret Service?"

"As insane as it seems, they're not required to protect presidential candidates," Deanne said. "After Dallas, I'm pretty sure they've had people watching Senator Kennedy, though."

"Then how could they screw up like this?"

Deanne shook her head.

"My guess – they were looking for a different threat," she said. "Something changed; they didn't react in time."

Gerald Portnoy barreled out of his office as the mayhem in Los Angeles played out before them all.

"Everybody listen up!" Portnoy shouted. "Complete reset. Everything on page one – gone. Tell me what we can get rid of. Now!"

"Maricopa Medical Examiner." Deanne said, blankly. It was a lame follow-up article that had barely crept it's way beneath the fold anyway.

"That's one. Come on people. Who's our man in Los Angeles?"

"Evans was." Sandy, their Controller said.

"What do you mean was?"

"He left for Chicago right after Kennedy won – to prep for the Democratic Convention," she said.

"Fuck."

"I can be there in six hours." Deanne said.

Portnoy practically spun on his heels to face her, for a moment it looked like he might explode.

"Gas is cheap," she said. "You won't eat a plane ticket. Gas, expenses, and the story. Politics and murder. I have the experience and you know it."

-=-=-=-=-

"Where the fuck were you last night!" Someone screeched.

As Deanne stepped, exhausted, into the Embassy Ballroom at the Ambassador Hotel, a long dark drive through the desert behind her, adrenaline depleted, and only the last remnants of her last cup of coffee holding her upright; the cry seemed to come from another world, as if someone somewhere outside this nightmare was trying to wake her.

The detritus of political celebration, the grand room with its chandeliers still blazing over bunting and confetti. Red, white and blue balloons, their helium mostly gone now, floated limply above the ribbons.

A blink was all it took to see the ghosts of last night's celebration – Robert F. Kennedy waving victoriously behind the podium, his adoring, pregnant wife behind him looking on with adoring but fretful eyes, eyes filled with the awful memories of Dallas. That beautiful moment before tragedy was imprisoned forever in history; like watching ghosts dance one last ball on the Titanic.

The cry echoed, *"Where the fuck were you, last night!"* and the ghosts faded.

She was back in the present, surrounded by LA County Sheriff's deputies, Ace Security guards, and men she deemed to be Secret Service; a day late, a Senator dying. On top of everything else, a terrible feeling of Déjà vu for Deanne.

"Get him the hell out of here," one of the men ordered, and two uniformed cops ushered the screaming young man roughly out of the ballroom.

"And what's she doing in here?"

The press credential she'd clipped to her blouse had gotten her this far – but it wouldn't get her anywhere near the service entrance behind the stage where the attack had taken place; not today.

A good-looking but haggard man, wearing a jacket and tie that might have looked crisp when he put it on some 24 hours ago, appeared from that hallway with several other men. His eyes traced the path Kennedy and his entourage likely took offstage toward the pantry; something he and the others had likely done a dozen times already since the attack.

He walked toward the entrance where Deanne stood, checking off the other possible exits and access points, and passed by as if she weren't there.

"Detective?"

"Press is down that hall," he said without so much as a glance her way. "Colonial room."

"What did he mean by that? 'Where were you?'"

The Detective straightened.

Deanne wasn't sure what she'd expect to see in his eyes when he faced her, anger, weariness?

Instead, an odd look of surprise.

Oddly, she became aware of herself; what she looked like right now. Droopy haired and colorless; she hadn't retouched her makeup. She'd barely stopped at her house long enough to throw a few more essentials into the travel bag she always carried in her trunk.

Jesus, why did any of that matter now?

A flush of heat swept her face. She'd definitely hit the wall.

"Um," he said, with the manner of a man unused to being at a loss, and then, the defenses, the anger came through.

"Talk to the Mayor."

-=-.=-.=-.=-

"For me, it's pretty much a toss-up," Ben said, as he and Sara prepared to move the customer onto his side.

"Being a big barbecue fan, I'd say dealing with crispy critters could turn me vegetarian..."

"One. Two..." Sara began.

"But floaters...well... that takes care of boiled cabbage and carrots."

"Three."

And the man was on his side. Several large flakes of charred skin from his back remained on the table behind.

"Be sure and collect those," Sara said.

"Got 'em."

Ben's question of which was worse to autopsy, floaters or crispy critters, in other words, drowning or burn victims, was the first attempt at banter he'd made today.

"I'll shut up," he said.

The morning had passed in relative silence, under a terrible cloud. While the rest of the shocked country waited with at least a glimmer of hope, within the LA County Crime Lab, preparations for the worst were already being made.

Some twelve hours after the attack, the news coming into the lab from Good Samaritan Hospital was the Senator, who had shown signs of improvement earlier, had taken a bad turn. He was rapidly losing his battle, and the inevitable was approaching.

The morning passed in a claustrophobic haze. For Sara, already drowning in her own pain, far from pulling her out of herself, the tragic news only amplified the very personal emptiness she felt inside.

If anything had been lifted from her, it was the very investigation that had kept her focused and moving forward. The mysterious and amorphous multiple murderer she and Deanne had been trying so desperately to identify had taken a backseat to everything.

Now, she had a brand new mystery on her hands.

At least cause of death and a pronouncement of foul play would be easy with the two customers they were currently examining.

A young man and an old woman had died together in a blazing car wreck. The man had been driving, if you could call it driving. His hands had been duct taped to the steering wheel. Charred bands of the material still hung from his broken hands.

Why the two were together, and who would choose to end their lives this way were the difficult questions – a task made even more difficult by the lack of identification found with either body.

The man's face was badly damaged. Neither occupant had worn seat-belts. The tape kept the driver's hands on the wheel, but did little to keep the rest of him from flying forward into the metal dash and windshield before the car caught fire.

As she carefully removed the tape from his right hand, she saw deep impressions just above the knuckle.

A row of semi-circular cuts. A bite-mark? Could it be? Or was that what she wanted to see? The tape had protected the area somewhat, but it was still badly damaged. Hard to tell for certain.

"Ben. Get a picture of that."

"You got it."

The bulbs flashed.

"Could be something he hit on the dash," he surmised.

"Could be. Or it could be a connection to Mr. Stumpy. No ID on either of these two. John and Jane Doe."

"The car was rented to a Milton Dowd – age 32, but this isn't him. Milton Dowd resides in a cemetery in Boston."

"Let me guess; stillborn?"

"Yup."

"Fake ID. Somebody went through a hell of a lot of trouble to set this up. Let's roll him back."

They eased him onto his back and Sara ran a quick visual check, top to bottom of what they had of him.

"Not seeing any identifying tats." She pointed to a raised patch of skin under his left armpit, another on his left bicep. "But tats might have been removed here, and here."

Ben's camera flashed.

"Maybe."

"Sharp muscular definition. This guy kept himself fit. Not a body-builder though. Low bulk and low body fat. I'm thinking martial arts; military or former military."

A couple dark scars cut deeply into his lower torso, one showed noticeable pitting at the perimeter.

"He's been shot before. Once at close range."

"So what's he doing with Grandma over there?"

"Maybe she is his grandmother."

"Maybe," Ben said, "but if she was, she's just visiting. Check out her clothes. Definitely 'old country.'"

Sara opened the bags that held what was left of their clothing. The man's slacks and shirt were contemporary and store bought, with machine stitched labels. The materials used for the woman's coat and dress were rough, inexpensive, but the stitching was carefully done. Hand-sewn.

"She made her own clothes," Sara said. "But not his."

"That doesn't mean they're not related. My grandmother makes some of her clothes. I get mine at JC Penney."

"Maybe you should rethink that."

"At last...Sara makes a joke. Is Sara back with the living?"

Sara barely heard him, instead her own grandmother's stories came through loud and clear; stories about traveling to the New Country. The woman and her family had shipped from Dorset traveling like cattle in steerage. With pickpockets and rogues everywhere, many women didn't trust carrying their personal items or money in a purse or pocketbook – if they could even afford such things. Instead, they'd sewn their valuables right into their clothes.

Sara flattened the burnt shell of the coat and ran her hands along the lining, sure enough, she felt a few thick patches in the charred seam.

"Ben – hand me the suture cutters."

She carefully cut the threads and opened the seam.

The remnants of burnt paper money slid out. A few thousand Russian Rubles and a photo, badly damaged by the fire. The woman in the photo looked to be the old woman herself. She stood next to a shapely young lady in a polka dot dress.

There was more.

Sara slid her gloved fingers into the seam and withdrew a folded patch of material; white with blue polka dots.

Material left over from her granddaughter's dress.

-=-=-=-=-

96

Sara ran to the phone in their break room at lunchtime. The notice of a call waiting for her on line 2 came over the intercom just as she reached it.

"Sara Poole."

"Deanne Mulhenney."

"Deanne! I was just about to call you! You sound close."

"I'm here in LA, at Good Samaritan. Well, across the street. You can't get to a phone over there right now."

"I have no doubt about that – work here has been non-stop. It's –"

"I know...like the entire country's been thrown out of balance."

"And every eye is on what we all do right now. When did you get here?"

"Around seven this morning – I drove."

"You must be ready to collapse."

"I think I did about two hours ago."

"You're staying with me, right?"

"I've got a room somewhere they call the Rampart District."

"Ugh. Like I say, you're staying with me."

When Deanne did get to the hotel, she checked in, showered, and fell asleep to the sounds of honking horns and sirens.

Four hours later, she woke abruptly to the sounds of honking horns and sirens.

Deanne quickly scanned the directions Sara had dictated to her house in Hermosa Beach. She checked them against the street map. The house was a long way from the action Deanne would be covering, but having that break might just keep her sane.

She decided to keep the hotel room as a base.

Deanne organized her notes and narrative. A quick check of local and national news revealed nothing new; Senator Robert F. Kennedy was holding on, if by a thread. The alleged shooter had been identified as a young Palestinian man with Jordanian citizenship. His name was Sirhan Sirhan.

No other suspects.

Deanne's first glimpse of the ocean took her breath away, as she drove her deep red Oldsmobile Starfire with its top-down into the little beach community.

The thin layer of fog drifting in only added another layer of calm and contrast with the pumped-up overdrive of Los Angeles she'd just left.

The temperature had dropped noticeably once she'd reached the coast. Coming from the blast-furnace of Phoenix and the concrete of downtown LA, it was actually chilly in Hermosa Beach. But the feeling was far from unpleasant.

She turned north just before the pier and parked only a few blocks away, tasting the brine of the marine air and wondering how she'd ever go back to Phoenix.

Moments later, purse and travel bag in hand, she stepped off the main road onto a path between two rows of bungalows.

Just a few doors down, Sara rose from a small table in her well-kept garden. She called Deanne's name over the distant boom of a crashing wave, popped open the low gate, and ran to her.

"Welcome to my world, friend!"

She dropped her bags and they hugged as it if had been years, not weeks since Deanne had watched Sara drive away.

Chapter 12

Maybe it had something to do with the low-key roar of waves in the background, the salty-sweet taste of the air or the deftly executed Manhattans; but as they sat in Sara's meticulously trimmed garden, pizza never tasted so good.

"Well, sans cooking skills, I figured this would work."

"You figured right." They clinked glasses. "Perfect pairing."

"Hah! Well, lately I've had some really bad influences in my life. Or one, at least. How long can you stay?"

"It isn't set, but not long. A few days. A week is likely a stretch. Depends what I find – more on what I deliver. Frankly, I think Portnoy is glad to have me out of his hair."

"Hey pretty girl, who's your pretty friend?"

A woolly old man appeared from a bungalow across the way, he picked up the surfboard that stood next to his door.

"Hey Bob," Sara asked. "You seriously going back out there now?"

"Ocean still there?"

"Far as I know."

"Then I'm going."

"This is Deanne – she's a reporter, so watch your p's and q's. Deanne, neighbor Bob. Best BBQ on that side of the path."

"Best on the beach!" He said without losing a step toward the water. "Reporter Deanne, you're here Saturday, you'll see. Pleased to meet you."

"The same." Deanne smiled as he continued on. "Well, there's some local color."

"Oh, there's plenty more around here believe me. Mostly harmless."

Deanne lifted her glass, watching the rays of sunset that pierced the fog play through the rust-colored fluid.

"I am a little surprised at these, I have to say."

"Well, let's just say I've come to understand some things lately."

"How do you mean?"

"I hurt someone. I mean...it balances out – I'm pretty sure I hurt myself more."

"Oh?" It wasn't what she'd expected to hear from Sara. But, thinking about it, it made sense. In the short time they'd known each other, they'd been through so much. Sara was strong, detached at times, but, like a lot of so-called still waters, Deanne knew Sara's emotions ran deep. Her detachment was a defense, and a well-practiced one.

Sara glanced out toward the rolling surf, and Deanne could sense her friend wasn't ready to take Deanne any deeper on this particular subject.

"Mr. Stumpy wasn't found that far from here. Want to take a walk?"

"Hard to pass up an invitation like that."

They walked barefoot in the cool wet sand. After a day in uncomfortable shoes, the giving embrace of it was just one more piece of heaven for Deanne.

The hazy red sun had nearly doused itself in the watery horizon, and lights began to flicker in the community above the beach.

"He was ID'd by the way," Sara said. "His name was Skip Morton."

"Doesn't exactly sound like a drug kingpin."

"Ad Man. Single. Squeaky clean."

"Jesus, of all the ways to end someone...who does that to Mister Squeaky Clean?"

"Someone like me who really, really hates commercials."

"Gambling debts?"

"Very possible. That could give him unwanted attention from the mob. Or big debts in general, depending on who he owed. Ad Men can be arrogant and showy – live well beyond their means. As you know..."

"Was that a dig?" Deanne asked. Deanne had gotten a bit too close to her subject while covering former advertising executive, Todd Worwick, during his campaign for senator. That mistake had nearly tanked the investigation and her friendship with Sara.

"Just pointing it out."

"Uh huh."

Sara looked up to the houses then took three long strides forward. She drew a line in the sand with her toe.

"He washed up right here."

Deanne looked back to the little concrete paths up to the bungalows, and the pier beyond.

"Not far from you at all."

"Very close. The question is, where did his last journey begin? The current along the coast flows south and inland. He spent a couple days in the water. To wind up here he was likely dropped a few miles north."

"Off a pier? Or a boat?"

"Well, the longest pier just north of here is Santa Monica. It's still too short – he'd have washed ashore right there, maybe Venice or Marina del Rey. Dumped from a boat would be my first guess"

Deanne considered that, finally, she shook her head.

"Unless someone saw the body being dropped, or just happened to come onboard later and see something suspicious, I'm guessing it could be a long time before any evidence turns up, if it ever does."

Sara nodded.

"So...while we wait for that never to happen...there's another possibility we can check out." She looked northwest into the fog up the beach. "It's tough to see right now, but going north, the coast angles gradually out into the water. If he wasn't dumped from a boat – to get all the way down here he'd have to have been dropped from a promontory, a point that juts way out into the ocean.

"And that gives us Malibu. Point Dume in particular."

-=-.=-.=-.=-

It was a small somewhat musty space, but as Deanne would have figured, Sara had made the most of the little bungalow with handmade pastel shelves and bright curtains. Beyond the den where she sat on a very comfortable woven couch, was a small kitchen area with a window surrounded by levels of potted plants and flowers, multi-color beaded curtains separated the kitchen from the bedroom and bath.

While the garden outside was certainly well-tended and trimmed to a handsome symmetry, the interior of the little house teamed with flowers, color and life. The feminine "prettiness" of it shouldn't have surprised Deanne, she supposed. Perfectly tanned and toned, with those wide and deep brown eyes and stylishly bobbed chestnut hair, Sara was pretty to the point of stunning – it was just that she rarely carried herself that way.

"Sorry for the mildew smell," Sara handed Deanne another Manhattan. "It comes with the territory. Most of these places should have been torn down years ago. But we're all hoping our landlord doesn't."

"A small price to pay for paradise," Deanne said.

Sara took another sip, she knelt in front of her album shelf, made a selection, and placed it on her turntable. Soon sweet music played softly. She turned on the television, twisted the sound down and adjusted the rabbit ears until a silent deathwatch of teary-eyed supporters at Good Samaritan appeared. Robert F. Kennedy was still holding on. The picture flicked from a rehash of the previous night, the campaign footage from the Ambassador Hotel, to Chicago where preparations were being made for the coming Democratic Convention, then back to Good Samaritan Hospital.

"If he dies...will you be involved?"

"From the sidelines, most likely. We get film stars and rock stars – but this is as high-profile as they get. The Chief will conduct the autopsy himself if it comes to that. Do you want to keep watching?"

"Doesn't look like anything new. I've had what I can take of it for one day. Being at the Ambassador this morning was surreal."

"No doubt. Oh, before I forget -" Sara produced a key from beneath a potted vine near the TV and handed it to her. "Take this. Things being as they are right now – my schedule could be up in the air."

She sat beside her on the couch and drew her legs up beneath her. They clinked glasses, and each took a long sip.

"I'm glad you're here, Deanne," she said.

"Me too. I wish the circumstances were better."

Deanne set her Manhattan on the coffee table next to Sara's.

"I'm enjoying these. Very well done by the way...but they take some practice to get right."

"Yeah. Well. Lately, I've been practicing quite a bit."

"Look, stop me if I'm crossing a line...but that's a big change for you.

"You said you hurt someone. You know you can talk to me."

Sara leaned back and took a breath.

"I do...and I will. It's just a little too close right now."

Deanne knew that feeling well enough. It wouldn't do any good to push. Not now. Instead, she just nodded, helpless to do anything more.

"Okay."

Sara unfolded herself and took the glasses to the kitchen.

"We should get some sleep – tomorrow's looking to be another long day. Fresh sheets on the bed. Coffee is right here next to the percolator, anything you find in the icebox and cupboard that isn't moving is yours."

"I'm fine out here on the couch. I don't want to put you out."

"Who said anything about a couch?"

Deanne stared at her and Sara laughed.

"I'm kidding. I've used it before, it's a pull-out. I'm good."

Sara stared out at the gauzy moon from her pull-out bed and listened to the rolling waves.

She gave Deanne high marks for staying awake as long as she had; not a peep from her now. It was odd how different everything felt from the moment she'd seen Deanne turn down her path, like things might just be all right.

She wasn't alone after all.

Sara blinked; she looked back to her record collection. A manila folder, *the* manila folder was tucked inconspicuously between two albums. She'd put Toxi-lab Tim's career, not to mention her own, on the line to get that report. And...just like that – life, and a would-be-assassin's bullet, had rendered it unimportant.

She'd almost pulled it out earlier tonight with Deanne – right after Manhattan #2, but she'd opted for *Procol Harum* instead.

It can wait until morning.

No. All signs pointed to one major cluster at daybreak.

She flicked on her reading light, pulled the folder and laid out the report on Meharis, the now-cremated movie mogul.

Fuck, you're an idiot.

She fought the urge to scream.

Right there in black and white: along with high levels of blood thinners and anti-hypertension drugs meant to keep his already damaged and clogged heart beating – MDMA and mega doses of caffeine. Molly and Guarana – enough to make his entire circulatory system explode.

The mogul was murdered using the same drugs and dosages found in Mr. Stumpy, the ad man.

How the hell was she going to sleep now?

She looked through the beaded curtains at Deanne's still form on her bed.

Let her sleep. Deanne's here to do her job. It's your fault you didn't do yours, not hers.

She'd let her awful mistake with Cromwell get to her and she'd dropped everything.

Raw heat rose in her throat; that urge to run naked into the waves and scream at the ocean, to beat something, someone to a pulp.

She walked stiffly to the kitchen, picked up the bottle of Jack Daniels and twisted off the cap.

Sara closed her eyes.

She took a deep breath. The air was sweet, tinged with the acrid bite of alcohol. She twisted the cap back in place.

She walked out into her garden, watched the tide pull back, and breathed in the salty mist.

After a few minutes, her head clear, she went back inside and read completely through the report, then something else caught her eye.

Ferric chloride heme. Teichmann's crystals.

"What the hell?"

There was something to that. Something from pre-med about red blood cells. Something *creepy*.

Given his bypass surgery, the idea that Meharis, the movie mogul, was taking blood thinners would be expected, but the presence of Ferric and Teichmann's meant something completely different was at play.

Her medical books sat peacefully on the shelves in her bedroom.

Deanne was dead asleep. What were the chances she could get to them without waking her?

She yawned.

Nothing she could do about it tonight anyway, and if she didn't get some sleep herself very soon, she'd never be able to make it through the next day.

Sara slid the report back into the folder and slipped it back in place between the album covers.

Sara crawled back under the sheet, puffed up the pillow and closed her eyes, feeling the soothing hands of sleep pulling her surely away to dreamland.

And then it hit her.

Robert F. Kennedy had died at 1:44 AM. The news blared from Deanne's radio the moment she'd flicked the radio on.

At 6AM, she'd given herself what she thought to be an early start. It was a long way to the freeway from Sara's house in Hermosa Beach, and coming from perfectly-gridded Phoenix, where nearly every strip of pavement ran north-south or east-west, navigating the side streets of Los Angeles was more art than science – an art she had little time to master.

She checked the street map as she drove, one eye on traffic that for this early hour was insanely heavy, wondering if she'd even survive the trip downtown.

Sara was out cold when Deanne left. Deanne wondered now if she should have tried to wake her. She had no idea what time Sara started work. No matter how much practice the girl had gotten in the last few weeks – she couldn't possibly have the alcohol tolerance Deanne had trained so diligently to build over the years.

This was going to be a heavy day for both of them. Press conferences at the hospital and City Hall and, now that the worst had been confirmed, Sara's boss, Chief Medical Examiner, Dr. Thomas Noguchi, was likely to be at one or both of them.

A truck running a red light just ahead of her, made Deanne slam her breaks – reminding Deanne her life depended on getting downtown safely. Sara was a big girl, after all.

Deanne's first plan was simple enough, go to Good Samaritan and then City Hall; cover the pressers, hear and see the "public" story.

The more she thought of that, the less value she saw in it.

The Associated Press was covering the pressers. The politically-staged "public" story would be out and endlessly repeated from the very moment the conferences began.

But the public story was rarely the true story. That story would be personal and painfully hidden; just as it had been with her investigation of abuse in the church, as it had been with the string of murders surrounding senatorial candidate, Todd Worwick.

Her friendship with Sara would give Deanne the unique advantage of hearing more than anyone would ever care to know about the grisly act of assassination.

But the story wasn't the act itself – it was what made that act possible...or necessary.

"Ask the Mayor."

That's what the detective had growled yesterday, as he gruffly brushed her off.

That was personal – that's where she needed to begin.

Deanne circled between City Hall, where cameras and microphones were already being set up and tested, and the LA County Jail, beginning to get her bearings, and a sense of the area.

The sheer size of Los Angeles was overwhelming. But given the size and easy weather, the foot traffic on the sidewalks was lighter than she would have imagined.

She parked as close as she could to the City Hall building, and started walking toward it. She'd barely touched the sidewalk when she saw the detective who'd blown by her yesterday at the Ambassador. At least, she was pretty sure it was him. Head slightly down, he was looking less disheveled but just as surly as he did then. He wore a different jacket today – same style, a darker gray – but this one hadn't been slept in. He was heading away from the gaggle of press gathered on the steps.

"Detective!" She called.

He slowed, though he didn't stop. She was somewhat surprised to see a flicker of recognition in his eyes.

She put out her hand; clear-headed today, this time her card was in it.

"Deanne Mulhenney, Arizona Tribune."

"So it says," he said, slowing just barely enough to read it. "The press —"

"Is setting up on the steps, I know. They were down the hall from the Embassy Room yesterday."

Finally he stopped walking. He turned back.

"I'm being an asshole," he said.

"A little bit."

His smile, half-smile that it was, changed the entire man; brought him from coarse to ruggedly good-looking. A handsome face that had taken a beating.

"Rick Cromwell, Detective LAPD." he said, handing her his own card.

"So it says."

"Well. Now that our cards have met, how can I help you, Miss Mulhenney?"

"I want to know what you meant yesterday. About the Mayor."

"That could take time I'm sure neither one of us has. If you're interested — he'll be right there on the steps with the Sheriff and Commish in half an hour."

"We both know how that will go, don't we? It's a terrible tragedy. The suspect is in custody, thanks to the fine work of everyone present here today. The city of Los Angeles is doing all it can to help our wonderful country heal. Then he'll step back and let the Sheriff and the Commissioner say the same thing in a slightly different way."

"You read the speech."

"Didn't have to."

"Didn't really think you did. But we both know you're right."

He continued walking.

"Are you headed to the jail?" She asked.

"To breakfast. I've had enough for now." He stopped again and sighed. He turned back to her. "Have you had yours? I'm buying coffee."

"No, I haven't. And sure." It took her a moment. "Let me guess...the coffee's free."

He grinned.

A short, hair-raising drive in his car later, and they were walking together toward the busy corner of Figueroa and 9th Street. It took her a moment to register all those people hanging out on the corner were waiting to get in.

"People actually wait in line outside for breakfast?"

"For *The Pantry?* Yeah, people actually do. You should see it at 3:AM. But, today, you're not people, you're *friend of police.*"

He turned just before the building, and then they were walking through a bustling kitchen, one of the few she'd ever walked through that didn't swelter in an overwhelming aroma of caked on grease and sour milk. The air tasted of sizzling ham and steaks.

Hard-looking older men in cardboard-stiff starched white shirts and black bow-ties passed by with white plates filled with enough meat, potatoes and, oddly, coleslaw to feed an army of lumberjacks.

Cromwell led her through the chaos, the two of them drawing barely a nod.

"Counter good?"

"Works for me."

Two places were cleared and they sat.

Humphrey Bogart walked by dressed in the same stiff white shirt and black tie as the others, Deanne's head swiveled.

"Good morning, Detective Cromwell," he said as he passed.

"Top of the morning, Bogie."

Deanne watched him take an order a few tables down.

"Could be his twin, right?" Cromwell said.

She nodded. "And he really goes by Bogie?"

"Who knows, in this city of dreams, maybe he really is Bogie."

A thick-boned man with hands the size of baseball mitts set two cups of black coffee in front of them, water and a pitcher of milk quickly followed.

"Your usual, Detective?"

108

"Sure."

"And the lady?"

She looked quickly up at the giant menu posted on the wall above him. And yes...the coffee was free.

"The steak and eggs. Medium rare. Sunnyside up."

"Good choice - I hope the lady's hungry..." Cromwell said.

"The lady is. Breakfast's on me, by the way."

"And flush too...maybe I should double my order."

"I have a per diem I'll never use. You're an expense."

"You're not the first to say that. So, Miss Mulhenney, I can't say I'm not enjoying the company, you've got sitting across from that little shit who pulled the trigger beat a hundred different ways – but what is it you're looking for? The facts in this case were clear once Sirhan's brother ID'd him. Everything I can tell you is likely out on the news-wires already."

"His brother? And please, call me Deanne. Can I call you Rick?"

"I've been called worse. Sure, Deanne."

"Let's start with what you're already putting out there."

"The suspect's name is Sirhan Sirhan. Born in Palestine, now a Jordanian citizen."

"And his brother identified him?"

"Yeah, he identified the .22 caliber pistol that appears to have been used."

"Why would his brother do that?"

"He's scared – and apparently doesn't share the same views, at least publicly."

"Okay. Palestinian – and the Senator was an outspoken supporter of Israel."

"Among other things. But without trying the kid before the actual trial, I think you can put 2 and 2 together – little Sirhan was not happy with the outcome of the 6-day War, and the Senator's support of it."

"And no other suspects? No broader conspiracy?"

"Leave that to the FBI – and Secret Service. They love that...stuff.

"No, we haven't completely ruled out other suspects – but the last thing we need are a lot of unsubstantiated rumors and conspiracy theories out there. If anyone else is involved – we'll need witnesses with raw facts. Conspiracies color recollections."

Mastodon-sized steaks and eggs arrived – with coleslaw on the side.

"Bon appetit, Deanne."

"Wow."

He smiled, sliced off a corner of his steak, swirled it in an egg yolk and chomped it down.

Deanne did the same, barely able to contain the growling in her stomach. It was perfect – delicious. She washed it down with hot coffee and her cup was immediately refilled.

"What is his mood?"

"Well, when I saw him – elated. Happy as Hell. That'll change once he sits in his cell long enough to figure out he's no hero and that cell is his new home."

"How involved will you be going forward?"

"Very little from here on. I'm on loan from the city. This is LA County's jurisdiction – until the FBI takes over, which is already happening."

"Any chance of my talking to him?"

"Zero to minus zero. No one wants another Lee Harvey Oswald. Security is tighter than a mouse's...well, it's tight."

"A lot more security than a presidential candidate gets. Certainly more than Bobby Kennedy had."

"Yeah. I guess you'd call that ironic. After this, that's likely to change too."

"When I talked to you at the Ambassador, it seemed like something more than irony."

Incredibly, even with all of the talk, Cromwell had nearly finished his breakfast – including the coleslaw. He swirled his last chunk of steak through the crusty remnants of yolk and downed it. He took a health swig of coffee.

"I guess this is where I say everything from this point on is off the record," he said.

"Noted. Is *unnamed source* okay?"

"You're a reporter, you have a job to do. Just keep in mind, mine is in this city. I have to work here after."

"I'll keep your name out of it."

He sipped his coffee, regarding that.

"I don't care for politics," he said, finally. "In the end, I don't know that it makes all that much difference which side gets in. Once they get there – they'll pretty much say or do anything to stay in. It's mostly BS as far as I can tell. But two nights ago we had a United States Senator running in a presidential primary. Not just any Senator, one who just might have made it – one whose brother did make it, and was assassinated for the honor.

"So let me ask you, Deanne. How many police do you think Los Angeles had protecting someone like that?"

"Judging by what that man shouted yesterday – not many."

"Zero. Nada. There was no PD at the Ambassador at all."

The admission was breath-taking.

"How...is that even possible?"

"It shouldn't be."

"It was politics? The Republican mayor of Los Angeles wouldn't protect a Democrat?"

"It's way beyond that. Republican-Democrat, sure, but that's a game. It was politics all right, but it was personal. Mayor Yorty and Senator Kennedy in particular."

He finished the cup, it was filled the moment it landed on the dish.

"Look, I like what I do...mostly. But lately...some things have happened. I'm not too sure of anything."

A question formed – and faded. Deanne had come to believe investigation was like a dance, sometimes you led. Sometimes it was better to follow. Now, she waited.

"How much do you know about the riots we've had here?"

"The Watts Riots? Sure. Blacks rioted over mistreatment by law enforcement, inequality."

"Yeah, well – that's the Reader's Digest version. Anyway it was messy and mean. Mean on both sides – but more than anything – it was LA's problem to solve. Bobby Kennedy made it the country's problem. Maybe he did it out of the goodness of his heart, or maybe he saw an opportunity to score points on the big stage. Whatever. He took it to the Mayor, made it personal, it turned into a dogfight... Look, you might have noticed, like most Angelenos – I'm not from here. Where I come from we know all about what happens when things get personal. People I grew up with call it *vendetta*. Vendetta or not – end result, no police protection on the biggest night of his life and Senator Kennedy is being autopsied as we drink our coffee."

Sara.

Sara was right there at ground zero, on the sidelines maybe, but they'd been preparing for the worst and the worst had happened. Dear God.

Focus.

The Mayor vs the Senator. Vendetta. That was the story. That was the perspective, the personal angle Deanne was looking for in all this.

"I don't know if any of that helps, Deanne. I need to get going. I'm sure you do too."

As they walked silently back to his car, something Cromwell had said earlier came back came to her.

"You mentioned the FBI and Secret Service – and conspiracy theories. Is that just interdepartmental rivalry talking, or is there something more to it?"

"Now you really want to get me in trouble don't you?" He smiled. "Why not throw the CIA in there too? Look, there's inside – close and personal; police, sheriff's office...and there's outside: big interstate, even international conspiracies– the stuff of UFO's and James Bond – that's where the FBI and CIA live. Secret Service, they get it from all sides – but they get hit harder from the CIA and FBI in my opinion – and they weren't charged with protecting a would-be nominee. Though we know that's gonna change."

"So there's a communication problem?"

"It's that, and it's a right tool for the job – hammer and nail kind of thing. If someone has a strong idea of what they're supposed to look for, do they really see everything? My experience is they only see what they're supposed to, or want to."

"You think there was something broader, and they missed it?"

"Maybe. I don't want to push that; the last thing we need are lunatics wasting our time. Maybe they thought they had something, maybe they were looking at the *wrong* something. In either case, they overlooked *close and personal* – a lone gunman with an ax to grind."

Another drive, made only slightly-less harrowing now that she was beginning to get a feel for the streets and where they were going, and Deanne thanked him for his time and candor.

"Okay if I call you with more questions?"

"You wouldn't call if I said, 'no'?" He grinned.

"Of course I would. I'm pretending to be polite."

-=-=-=-=-

It was a crusty bar not far from the point where Sara said the ill-fated ad man had washed ashore. As Deanne approached the entrance of Shanty's, she changed that to *encrusted*. Actual barnacles – long dead, she hoped but couldn't assume, were still attached to many of the thick beams used in its walls. It was a place she might expect to see the ghosts of shipwrecks past at the bar – or maybe next-door-neighbor, Bob the surfer, not Sara.

But there Sara was, sitting alone, but clearly not unnoticed by the weathered men sitting further down the bar. When she waved Deanne over, the men looked Deanne over stem to stern, apparently decided she too was sea-worthy, and nodded to each other.

Sara handed Deanne a Manhattan as she slid off the stool and headed for a booth off in a particularly dark corner of the dimly lit restaurant area, "you may want some food too."

"These are a good start."

"Believe it or not, the fish and chips here are great."

"Wouldn't have guessed."

Sara collapsed into her chair.

"God, where do I begin?"

"With a toast. We both survived this day."

Their glasses clinked.

"So far," Sara said, wearily, "so far, I'm not making any bets from this point on. Couldn't even think about cooking – lucky for you. Glad you got my message about this place."

"The two at the hotel and the one on your refrigerator. My day was an overload – I can't imagine what yours was like."

"I can't even say…" In one gulp Sara finished what Deanne hoped was only her first Manhattan of the evening, she ordered another and they both opted for the fish and chips.

Sara drew her shoulders up tight and then, closed her eyes. She took a deep breath. Finally, she settled into the booth, practically melted into it.

"Today was…gut-wrenching."

"God, you were *part* of it."

"Assisted, but…" She shook her head. "At least it's over now, he's on his way home."

"Just like that."

"Just like that. I know. Hard to find perspective there… In the end, I guess that's how it will be…for all of us."

"Did…anything point to more than one shooter?"

"No. Not really. The fatal shot struck behind his right ear, close range. Odd angle for the way he was approached – the witnesses so far say the shooter was in front of him."

"I'm sure some folks will try to make hay out of that."

"I'm sure they will. But in a crowd of people vying for attention – all the senator had to do was turn his head to talk to someone else." She turned her head to the left and tapped just behind her right ear.

"Have they even started forensics on the bullets yet?"

"There's priority – and then there's this. More to be done but initial results point to all slugs being fired from the same weapon – the .22 caliber they pulled from him at the scene."

"Hard to imagine something that small being used in a professional hit. Seems like you'd be cutting down your chances of success."

"Up close and personal they can cause a lot of damage, obviously. But you're right - unless they were absolutely certain of getting a shooter that close."

"Close and personal…" Deanne repeated. "Fits in with something I heard today."

"How's that side of the story coming?"

"I think I found the right angle – the personal side, Yorty and Kennedy."

"Whew. That won't be popular in these parts."

"No…lots of push-back already. I spent a good bit of time trying to get someone, anyone in the Mayor's office to talk about it."

"You went straight to the Mayor's office with that? You're a braver man than I."

"Hah! Well, if there's any good to any of this, Portnoy likes my take. It bought me a few more days."

They toasted.

"Good girl."

Sara took another deep breath, another sip, and seemingly for the first time tonight, took notice of the shipwreck they seemed to be sitting in. She shook her head.

"I can't believe I had you meet me here of all places."

"It does seem a little salty for you."

Sara laughed, somewhat sadly, it seemed to Deanne. "There are definitely cooler hangs to show off, I think I just...I'm not even sure what I thought. Anyway, dinner's arrived."

For the second time today, Deanne was pleasantly surprised at the offering. The plate of crispy cod and chips was like manna from the heavens. Of course, being famished didn't hurt. Nothing like tragedy and autopsy talk to whet the palate. Jesus, what was she turning into?

She thought about Detective Cromwell. In the midst of all of this, she had to admit she'd enjoyed their strange morning together. Enjoyed it a lot.

Sara dabbed a healthy chunk of fish in a cup of tartar and downed it like it was her first meal. Knowing the way Sara threw herself into her work, it likely was her first meal of the day. Deanne had to smile, if anyone could look perfectly beautiful eating like a wild horse – Sara could. Amazing.

"That's better..." Sara said, taking a quick breather.

"Look. We have to talk about the other case."

"Mr. Stumpy?"

"Poor soul has carried that name to heaven."

"Only with us – hopefully."

"Stumpy and Maharis. They were murdered by the same killer."

"How do you know? What's changed?"

"I've had the evidence for days. I sat on it. It was right there in the toxicology reports and I couldn't be bothered to read them."

"The whole country's out of whack right now, it's not your fault."

"No...I let other things...distract me."

"Catch me up. What do you have?"

"The bite marks and the drugs. Both men were injected and overdosed with the same odd mix of psychoactive drugs in the same proportions. And there's more – artifacts of another drug that wasn't meant to be injected but showed up in both reports."

"Wasn't meant to be?"

They went silent as the waitress took their plates. Then ordered another round of Manhattans without hesitating.

She waited until the waitress was clearly out of earshot.

"I'm certain it came from the killer's bloodstream, not theirs. Hydroxy chloroquine."

"What the hell is that?"

"I had to check my medical books. It's used to treat porphyria. The disorder's rare, as in maybe one in fifty-thousand people have it. The chances both our victims would have it are next to none. And neither man did have it, their blood cells were relatively normal at the time of death."

"So, you said the drug showed up in both men, what makes you think it wasn't just mixed in with the other drugs and injected?"

"Good question – a tiny part was –"

They stopped long enough to greet the arrival of the next round.

"Without getting too far in the weeds about the metabolization and breakdown of hemin and the presence of Teichmann's crystals –"

"I appreciate that."

"Most of the evidence came from swabs taken from Maharis's nether regions. Whatever fluids may have been on Stumpy washed off in the ocean. We found a very tiny bit in both bloodstreams – and that likely did come from a contaminated syringe."

"So we have a single killer – a female, apparently an extremely good-looking one from our witnesses at the studio – who suffers from perif -"

"Porphyria."

"Yeah, that. What is it?"

"Think of those odd marks – the all-too-perfect bite wounds. Victims of Porphyria have a deficiency in their red blood cells. In the worst cases they literally need an external blood supply to survive."

Deanne looked Sara dead in the eye, hoping to find at least a trace of humor there. There was none.

"She's a *vampire?*"

116

"Kind of. Not the Bram Stoker-Bela Lugosi kind."

"There's another kind?"

"What she has is a disorder, not some darkly romantic super power."

"You're telling me vampires are real?"

"It's likely porphyria inspired the legend. Have you heard of Elizabeth Bathory?"

"Hungarian royalty. Late 1500s. I know she was a murderer."

"Yes. The most prolific female multiple murderer in history. She killed hundreds – girls mostly. They called her *Blood Princess*. She literally bathed in their blood. They say she drank it."

"And she had porphyria?"

"It's believed she did. That would have given her the need for blood, possibly even the taste for it."

"Or she could have been insane."

"There's that."

"But it's a disorder, not a disease? It doesn't spread?"

"Well...that's the good news. It's genetic, abnormal. A mutated, re-ordered bit of DNA that gets passed down."

"Her parents were vampires?"

"One or both carried the gene, but they may not have known they had it. It could have sat dormant in the family for generations – or something catastrophic reordered their DNA."

"What causes DNA to...reorder?"

"Over time, malnutrition, adaptation to very harsh environments. But one generation? It would have to be exposure to extremely high levels of radiation."

Deanne set down her cocktail. She would never see it quite the same way again.

"The Manhattan Project."

Chapter 13

"Good God, girl! You are going to be the death of me."

Alena stroked him ever so lightly, the shaft stiffening surely once more as she guided him to her.

He gasped.

"I'm not...exactly...in my twenties..."

She shushed him, smiling, her powerful thighs held her just above him, just close enough for her to feel the warmth rising from him. Spread beneath them were the furs of wolves he'd killed, their touch was an animal mix of smooth and rough that both satisfied and provoked her.

Harry Champlain's silver hair matched the color of the fur. She ran her lips lightly down his cheek, feeling him shudder as she opened her mouth to taste his skin, her teeth so lightly tickling his jugular vein.

She impaled herself swiftly and smoothly, reveling in the explosion of heat deep inside her.

"God!" He cried.

Fresh from the shower, she greeted him at the windowed nook in his wide, open bedroom with a kiss. From here, she could just make out one far-off corner of her house beyond the trees. It was a concern she filed away for now.

Harry set his newspaper down and returned the favor of her morning kiss. The look on his face was one caught somewhere between pure joy and absolute disbelief.

She had seen that look before...in her victims.

"Don't look at me that way," she said.

"Oh. I'm sorry..." He frowned, but nodded. "I shouldn't presume
_"

She softened her look, or tried to. She smiled, sweetly, she hoped.
"What are you reading?"
He sat back in his chair.
"The Kennedy thing. The assassination."
"Tragic," she said.
"Well. I can't say I cared for him. But yeah, nobody wants that."
Alena nodded.
"Anything new?"
"Not really. Lone gunman, but you know they're bound to come
up with a thousand different conspiracies, like they did with his brother."
"Americans love our conspiracies."
"Yes we do. Here's one thing though. A piece in the Times quotes
an article from some paper in Arizona. Some reporter puts the blame on a
lack of PD at the Ambassador that night. Hah! Sam Yorty's not gonna like
this."
"Arizona?"
"Yeah. Heck, I know Sam. Good man. Solid Republican. Not too
many folks here'd want to piss him off. Leave it to a Zonie."
"Can I see that?"
"Sure." He pulled the sports section and handed her the rest.
"Shame about Drysdale – he pitched the game of his life the same night
Kennedy got shot. THAT should have been the headline. Talk about bad
timing..."
"Timing is everything," she said.
Alena scanned the article. Sure enough, it cited another from *The
Arizona Tribune*. That article's focus on a lack of protection at the kill site
was correct. No mention of a wider conspiracy. She noted the reporter's
name; Deanne Mulhenney.

-=-=-=-=-

Located on the wide, busy Pico Boulevard in West Los Angeles, The Apple
Pan restaurant looked like a tiny white house.

A tiny white house that smelled delicious, like baked apples and grilled burgers. Deanne would be taking more than her stories back home with her, about ten pounds more she figured.

She saw Cromwell seated at the counter the moment she stepped inside. He smiled broadly as he turned the padded seat beside him for her.

"Thanks for taking my call," she said.

"Did you think I wouldn't?"

"There's always that chance. Certainly the Mayor's office has been less than polite."

"Comes with the territory, doesn't it?"

"Yes, it does."

"Oh, if you like it smokey, go with the hickory burger. On me today. Pie too."

"Really?" She looked up to the big man in the white apron. "I'll be going with the hickory burger."

The man quickly jotted it on his pad.

"Coffee?"

"Sure."

"Pie?"

"Apple."

"The lady makes good choices once again," Cromwell smiled. "Although, I gotta say the coconut cream is worth taking a bullet for."

"Hmm. I really don't picture you as a coconut cream pie sort've guy."

"See, you don't know me. I'm what you'd call, multi-layered."

"Ah," she smiled, tipping the little white pitcher into her cup. The milk coagulated the moment it touched the black coffee. "Say, this is actual cream."

"Yes it is. There's a trick to it. Let me show you. Hey, Bud, can we get a fresh cup over here?"

"You got it."

Cromwell took her spoon as the fresh, steaming cup arrived.

"You just touch the spoon to the coffee, tilt the spoon like so...and pour into the spoon." He swirled the cream smoothly into her cup.

"You learn something new every day."

"Trick is to warm it, not scorch it. Like an omelet."

"You cook too?"

"I don't know if I'd call what I do cooking. More of a survival technique."

Thick juicy burgers arrived, wrapped in paper.

"That was fast."

"Fast and fresh. You go first."

It was all she could do to get her jaw around it. When she bit down, hickory sauce and the hamburger juice squirted down her cheek.

He laughed.

"Oh my god, this is delicious. No way to do this like a lady," she said, pressing her napkin to her cheek.

"No. I don't suppose there is. I wouldn't worry."

"Then stop laughing," she said, laughing herself.

He munched into his, with similar results.

"That's why I waited. I didn't want to look, you know, unsophisticated in the lady's presence."

"Hah! Thanks a lot!"

She chased it with half a glass of water.

"I may need a Coke."

"I should check with the bank, but I think I can swing that – can we add a Coke over here?"

The sugary fizz felt good. A few sips and she could speak clearly again. She felt good, weirdly, like one of the better days in high school.

"Lest I forget why I called. I want to follow up...and get your take on something else."

"I had a feeling you weren't just looking for another fine dining experience. Actually, I have something to ask – something you could help with."

"Oh. That's intriguing. You first this time."

He laid a few bills on the counter. "Mind walking this off with me?"

"Not at all. It's a nice day."

"They usually are," he almost seemed disappointed when he said it.

And a beautiful, sunny day it was. As they walked along the street, the shade trees were surprisingly welcome.

"Okay. It's most likely nothing," Cromwell said. "But it could be important. We've had two separate witness accounts of a young girl that might, and I put heavy emphasis on the word might, have had contact with our shooter the other night just prior."

"Really? Contact...as in accomplice?"

"I don't want to go there – not yet. Right now, we'd just like to talk to her – if she even exists."

"Anything special about her? Distinguishing features."

"Very...shapely, especially on top."

"Big bosomed?"

"Yeah, and pretty face. Not sure of the hair color, different accounts there – dirty blonde, brown. She was wearing a white dress with polka-dots – that's consistent. Possibly blue polka dots, maybe black – but there were a number of girls with polka-dot dresses at the Ambassador that night."

"And people saw her with Sirhan Sirhan? Were they talking?"

"Well, that's the thing – the witnesses say they were just standing close, not talking. It was more of a strong impression they were together. Like I say, it could be nothing. But here's the kicker. One of the witnesses nearly got knocked over by a girl in a polka dot dress running out while most folks were running in. The girl supposedly said, "We shot him.""

"That sounds like a pretty clear connection to me."

"It does – but it could also mean 'we the country,' which is the way one witness heard it. We don't know the intent."

"Jesus. That's still huge."

"Again, to be clear, we don't know the intent. We don't even know if it's the same girl. Until we talk to her, we won't know anything."

"So you'd like it out there the authorities want to talk to a girl who wore a polka dot dress to the Ambassador that night – one who might have been close enough to have seen something?"

"Something like that. If she exists, she's a witness, that's all. Like I said, conspiracies color recollection. That's exactly what we don't want."

Deanne nodded.

"Okay. I can live with that for now. Just be honest with me."

"I'll tell you what I can. That's all I can promise."

"You can't promise you'll be honest?"

"It's an open investigation, Deanne."

She considered that.

"Okay, Rick," she said. "I have something to ask you – a case completely unrelated to the assassination."

"Arizona case?"

"An LA case that might tie to one a bit south of our border. Sinaloa."

"Sinaloa? That's more than a bit south of Arizona. I'm intrigued. Which LA case?"

"Skip Morton."

"Whew..." He straightened.

"How much do you know about it?"

"Enough not to want to see another one like it. No head, hands or feet. Washed up south of here. What's your case?"

"Similar outcome – all identifying features removed like Morton, but he was identified eventually. His name was Vincent Romano, former member of the Borrono crime organization."

"Borrono."

"You've heard of them?"

"I'm from New York."

"Any chance Morton knew them? Drugs? Gambling debts?"

"You sure you're not a cop?"

"Is that a yes?"

"Squeaky clean."

Hearing that term again made Deanne smile.

"So I've heard. A good-looking advertising exec with a big agency. Unmarried but certainly eligible. He met a pretty brutal end for someone with nothing to hide, don't you think?"

"You've done some homework on this."

"I'll take that as you're still looking into it."

He nodded.

"...and it's an open investigation, I get that. Come on, Rick. I'm doing you a solid, I'll get the word out about Miss Polka-dots. We can help each other here. Was he at work the day he disappeared?"

"Yeah. He was distraught – lost out on a big promotion that day."

"Any bars he frequented?"

"He was an ad man. Very few he *didn't* frequent."

"It's a big city."

"He was a thirsty guy. We've checked out his usual hangs. All no-shows that night. He was pissed off with work, in no mood to drink with his office buddies."

"So he strayed outside his normal circles looking for a little ego boost – and picked someone up, or was picked up by someone. Skip had some very rough sex just before he was murdered – same with Vincent."

"How do you know all this?"

"Don't expect me to tell you. I shield my sources, like the law says I can. You're a source now, if you don't believe I'd do that for them, why would you think I'd do it for you?"

"That's a tough cookie under all that sugar."

"I'll take that as a compliment."

"It is. Okay. We've moved the search to a few communities on the west side. Malibu, Brentwood, the Palisades – and then south – Manhattan Beach and Hermosa Beach in particular – near where he was found."

"But you don't think the area between Manhattan and Hermosa is where he was dumped?"

"He may have met a woman in that area, but we don't believe that's where he entered the water."

"The current flows southeast."

"Yes." He looked sideways at her, "That it does."

"Doesn't that make Malibu your best choice?"

Once again he gave her a look.

"A good one anyway – if he wasn't dumped out of a boat."

They'd walked up one side of the street and down the other, and as they reached his car he hesitated. Deanne saw a flicker of something in his eyes, a question meant to be asked, reconsidered, then just as quickly dropped.

"Well, once again, it's been a pleasure, Miss Mulhenney."

"So we're back to formal now, Detective?"

He grinned as he popped open his door. "Just jerking your chain."

"Hmmph. I do have another question."

"Shoot."

"Why are you looking in those specific communities?"

"Morton took out a sizable loan the same week he was murdered – now don't get too excited about a Mafia connection there yet – the loan was from a bank, not sharks. His friends say he'd been looking at houses in those areas, really nice ones. He was counting on that promotion to make his move."

-=-=-=-=-

"The spook's not going to like what you're doing, Tony."

Gino Taglia, a slight man with a big camera, shook his head as he blew lint off the long lens. He rubbed the glass shiny and clean with the tail of his shirt.

"Yeah, well fuck her." Tony the Hammer Buldoni checked the tree next to him. Satisfied there was no running sap to ruin his jacket, he leaned his bulk against it and readjusted his binoculars.

His circle of vision pulled in, bringing the two hazy forms beyond the window into sharp focus. The alien bitch was straddling Mister Mustache again.

"Like fuckin' rabbits, these two. Day after fuckin' night. You gettin' this?"

"Yeah." The camera clicked and clicked again. "I think you like it."

"Fuck you too. That mustache's old enough to be her fucking Nono. Madonna!" Tony spat for emphasis. He wiped his lips with his sleeve. "That's enough for now. I wanna eat again someday."

Driving Tony's Lincoln back down Mandeville Canyon Road, Gino squinted into the rear-view at the big man. He and Tony went way back. Tony maybe wasn't the sharpest tool, but he was ruthless, ambitious and shrewd enough to tie in with Toro Borrono when that family moved up. Loyalty was bread and butter; but it wasn't blood.

Trusted soldiers as they were, they weren't family.

"You sure you're not just gonna piss the old man off doing this? I mean, Alena's like his niece or something."

"The Aliena's not related to nobody. She wasn't even born – she was, you know, hatched. Like from a chicken egg."

Gino laughed.

"That hen must've been a looker."

Tony spat out the window this time.

"You seen her without a wig – all that makeup? Oof!" Tony pretended to shudder.

"You have?"

"No. But I've heard stories," he backtracked. "I hear she's a toothless, bald – alba...whatchacallit."

"Albino?"

"Yeah. That."

Gino smirked into the rear-view.

"All I can say is I've taken a whole lot of pictures – all I see is one hot little tomato."

"Don't make me gag."

"So now do we get some breakfast?"

Tony checked his Rolex.

"Now we make that drop in Brentwood. Then...we get breakfast."

-=-=-=-=-

The cigar stub smoldered at the edge of the crystal ashtray next to Toro Borrono's drumming fingers. A big chunk of ash sheared away from it like the business end of a glacier, sending a wave of hot powder across the deeply polished desk.

"Marie!"

He turned over the sickening photos as the maid rushed in. She quickly brushed the ash into a pan, and rubbed away the scorch mark.

"Grazie, Marie."

The young woman gave a quick bow, pausing only long enough to smile at Johnny Handsome on the way out.

Johnny's wink flushed her cheeks.

Toro rubbed his forehead. He left the photos face down.

"Johnny. Why the fuck did you show me this fugatz? You think I want to see this?"

Johnny shook his head.

"Dad, it hurt me to see it. You know I love her like a sister. It hurts me to bring it to you."

"Tony took these pictures didn't he? That sick fuck."

"It doesn't matter where they came from. It's a problem."

"If I had someone follow Tony around with a camera, you don't think he'd have a problem? What about you, Johnny?" He looked up at the door the maid had just closed. "In my own house – you think I don't know what goes on? You're a married man."

Johnny straightened.

"We're talking about Alena. This isn't...normal for her – it's not what she does...she's getting careless."

"Fuck you know?"

"All feelings aside, I know what makes her valuable to this family is she's precise and she's invisible. Like a secret weapon. Even more than that - she's always been our secret weapon. Lately, I'm not so sure."

Toro looked directly into his son's eyes. Johnny knew that look. Tread softly.

"You come back to me with more than you're not so sure and I'll bring her in for a sit-down."

Johnny nodded.

"And tell Tony, I appreciate his concerns, but he takes any more naked pictures of Alena he'll be choking on his own balls."

-=-.=-.=-.=-

Sara hadn't lost her edge.

It had taken a solid hour of kicks to the body bag, innumerable strikes against the makiwara to sweat out the sins of alcohol and malaise she'd inflicted on herself. But Sara was back.

Still pumped from her first workout since the debacle with Rick, her footfalls were dancer light as Sara bounced her way down the walk; her legs were springs. Bob stopped pouring charcoal briquettes from a big bag just long enough to wave. He'd built his barbecue from an oil drum. A tower of cinder blocks beside it would soon hold a gigantic block of ice down which would run a seemingly endless river of booze.

Tomorrow was Barbecue Saturday in Hermosa Beach, and Deanne was in for a treat!

Even over the rolling waves she heard the machine-gun rat-a-tat-tat of Deanne hard at work, the lights were on at home – and, what was that, the sweet aromas of garlic and basil in the air?

Had Deanne cooked dinner?

Life was good. Could it always be this way? Why not?

She effortlessly hopped her own gate.

"Hey friend!" Deanne chirped from the floor, her back against the couch, her legs protruding beneath the coffee table – a pile of balled-up typing paper sat beside the typewriter, a bottle of red wine and two glasses beside that.

Sara bent and kissed Deanne's cheek.

"Honey, I'm home." She laughed.

"… and dinner's warming in the oven. Lasagna and garlic bread."

"Smells like heaven. I'm famished.'

"And no...I didn't cook it. I cheated and bought it down the street. Just finishing up here. Pour yourself a glass."

"Hah! I think I'll skip that tonight."

"You on the wagon?"

"Until tomorrow at least. I don't think it's possible to make it through Barbecue Saturday without at least one ice shot."

"Yeah – I took a walk earlier. Quite the setup going on out there. Is it always like this on the weekends?"

"Way more often than healthy."

"Got your message. You worked out – good for you."

"Too long neglected. Much needed. Just going to jump in the shower and let's eat!"

"Hey – I hope it goes without saying, but don't let me break your schedule, I'm very self-sufficient."

Sara twisted on the hot water, dancing away from the cool spray. She poked her head beyond the curtain.

"I know you are."

But the typing had already re-started in earnest. It made Sara smile.

Freshly showered, toweled and still wrapped in her endorphin afterglow, Sara set two plates of lasagna on the kitchen table and lit two candles.

"Take a break, let's eat."

"I just called my update in." Deanne sighed, "Not the best job of word-smithing...but it'll do for now." She extricated herself from beneath the coffee table and took the bottle and glasses with her to the kitchen.

"Sure you don't want one of these?"
Sara held up a tall glass of water.
"Gonna stick with this tonight. I'm proposing a field trip in the morning."
"And miss Barbecue Saturday?"
"Short trip. We'll be back before the first drunk falls."
"Let me guess – up the coast to Malibu?"
Sara nodded.
"Yeah, I think we might hike up Point Dume."
"Hah. And here I was thinking you might need a break from all this."
Sara savored her first bite. She took a long sip of water.
"We both do. Tomorrow's the best time to do it, though. I don't expect either of us will be of much use Sunday morning."
"I did learn a few things about Mister Stumpy today."
"Nooo…you'll ruin lasagna for me, forever!"
Deanne laughed, "Okay, no more shop talk tonight."
Sara raised her water glass.
"To a relaxing evening of just us."
Deanne clinked her full balloon glass to it.
"So…how early are we talking?" She nearly spit red wine across the kitchen when Sara answered,
"Just before sunrise."

-=-=-=-=-

Sometimes it's good to be nothing but the sleepy passenger. Deanne was thoroughly content with Sara at the wheel. The sun was barely rising as Sara pulled her car off the main road. The drive up here, the views of the ocean as the first flecks of sunrise lit the water had been nothing short of spectacular.

They had come to a small beach area protected by high cliffs – the southern wall jutted out into the sea. It was cut with narrow footpaths. The secluded cove with the wide ocean beyond was beautiful, and somehow eerie and alien at the same time.

"They film here sometimes." Sara said as she pulled to a stop. "Some of that new movie, *Planet of the Apes*, was shot here."

Deanne could easily picture that.

"That was an odd book. Good...but odd."

"Pierre Boole, right."

"Yeah."

They sat for a moment, saying nothing.

Intuition is a good thing, but it can often be disturbing.

Without a word between them, they spoke to each other.

He was here.

Sara reached into the glove compartment, retrieved a flashlight, a roll of plastic bags and a packet of disposable latex gloves.

"Could you grab my camera bag?"

Deanne reached over her seat and pulled the strap over her shoulder.

"Got it."

The sun was only beginning to fill in the shadows as they worked their way up the rocky cliff-side; Sara swept the paths and the rocks beside them with her flashlight.

As secluded as the area was, there were plenty of footprints. Sara groaned.

"I should have been up here days ago. This is a major make-out destination. Any evidence..."

She shook her head.

"Wait."

The disk of light followed a wide track in the sand between the rocks. Footsteps had nearly obliterated it – but it was there. Something large and heavy had been dragged up here. On either side of that track, rocks had clearly been rolled or pushed to one side.

Deanne pulled the camera from the bag, framed and shot it.

Sara nodded.

"Get a few shots of that."

Sara moved forward quickly, pulled on a pair of gloves and shook out one of her evidence bags.

"And here."

Deanne would never have noticed the small, dark clots of sand. Deanne focused and shot.

Sara carefully gathered a few of them into her bag. She pulled a grease pen from her pocket and scratched some numbers on the side.

"This is a crime scene now. You know the drill."

Sara moved as far to the other side of the path as possible, and Deanne did the same, following her friend up and between the rocky outcroppings toward the sea, to the exact spot where the mutilated body of a former advertising executive, had been dumped like so much trash into the surf below.

Finally, they reached the highest point.

Just below them, a tall man stood at the very edge of the cliff, looking into the waves crashing below.

"Rick?" Deanne said.

Sara met Deanne's surprised expression with one of stunned disbelief...and pain. For a moment, Deanne was afraid her friend would either collapse – or run.

Rick said nothing when he turned toward them, but Deanne saw him take a quick breath.

"I think I hurt someone, badly. I think I hurt myself even more."

Sara had said that, hadn't she?

Chapter 14

"I had no idea..."

"I know you didn't. It's not your fault. You asked me what was wrong...I never told you what I did. I...couldn't."

Deanne felt Sara's pain in her own heart. Their friendship was short in terms of time, but already deep in shared emotion and tragedy. Without a doubt, Sara was one of the strongest people Deanne knew.

But she kept so much inside. And it wasn't until they'd left the short, awkward encounter with Rick Cromwell at Point Dume and begun their drive home that Sara broke and told her...everything.

Sara shook her head slowly, a white-knuckled grip on the wheel as she drove them into the city; her cheeks still wet with tears she'd wiped away only moments before.

"I've got to sign these in at the lab. We'll be back at the beach –"

"Before the first drunk falls. I know."

Sara nodded, "I'll be over this, don't worry."

Deanne couldn't remember a moment when the idea of a drunken beach party could have meant less to her. As hard as it was seeing Sara hurt, the pang of guilt she felt being part of that hurt made it worse – even though she'd done nothing wrong. She'd flirted with a good-looking man, part of that had been reflex, she was attractive and being so was a useful tool with men and women alike, she accepted that. As an attractive man, he'd done the same right back. Still, their conversations had been more than just two people probing for information. She wasn't stupid.

Just before Cromwell had driven off yesterday, a question was there in his eyes and she knew exactly what that question was; *would she care for lunch, a drink, another meeting that had nothing to do with casework?* At the last moment he'd changed gears and stopped himself. But what if he'd actually asked that question?

She'd have said, "yes." In a heartbeat.

-=-=-=-=-

"Arizona Tribune, how may I help you?"

"I need to speak to Deanne Mulhenney. I have information she's looking for."

"I can take that information for her."

"I'm afraid it's extremely sensitive. Perhaps we could meet. Is she still here in Los Angeles?"

"Miss Mulhenney's..." the hesitation was slight, but telling, *"...in the field, if you'll give me your number —"*

Chumo opened the big phone book, he read back the first number that appeared above his index finger.

"I'll make sure she gets this."

"Thank you."

Alena, wearing a wide-brimmed hat and dark glasses, sat in the back seat of their car next to the newsstand across the street. She looked up from her own fresh copies of this morning's Arizona Tribune and The Los Angeles Times as he crossed over.

"She's still here," he said confidently.

"Good."

"Library?"

She glanced quickly up at the bright, rising sun.

"Yes. Perfect day for it."

Today, Mulhenney's article on the assassination included a request for information concerning a young woman in a polka-dot dress who "may have witnessed the assassination."

That request was interesting and astute, but not a concern in itself. The informant had been removed before she could flag the threat, and the target had been removed. Chumo and Alena had done their jobs. There was nothing to connect them.

It was a separate Mulhenney article further down the page that had caught Alena's attention. The story suggested a possible link between what Mulhenney described as "two horrific murders thousands of miles apart." The murders of Vincent Romano and Skip Morton.

The linking of those two names had caused a flicker of something Chumo had never before seen in Alena's pale, beautiful eyes – a level of concern bordering on panic.

But that moment had been fleeting. She was back in her usual mode of calm calculation. She spoke as casually now as someone reciting the latest minor league baseball scores.

"The Times hasn't picked up that story...yet."

Chumo nodded, "It buys us some time."

The unspoken "unspeakable" that hung in the air between them was the effect this development could have on the Borrono family, and their relationship with it. Mafia hits like the murder of Vincent Romano, while certainly investigated and prosecuted, were treated by the authorities as something of a self-cleansing, one less *gumba* on the streets. Not a priority. However, collateral damage connected to the mob, as Morton would be seen, was another matter entirely.

And if Morton could be connected...others would soon follow.

"This article is somewhat sensational," Alena said. "She focuses on the way the bodies looked when they were found. If she has any real forensic information, she's holding those cards."

"She probably hasn't seen anything like *that* in Arizona," Chumo offered. "She needs to travel."

"Yet neither body was found there." Alena folded her arms, she looked out the window to the camera-toting tourists tramping the sidewalks, up to the palm-laden hills of Hollywood beyond. "That's the question we need to answer, Chumo. Why would a reporter from an Arizona newspaper be interested in either one? What exactly is her connection?"

-=-=-=-=-

Gray images flickered as Alena rolled through pages of microfiche; she stopped just long enough to frame, focus and quickly read the articles. Within thirty minutes she had a feel for the young woman whose face appeared beside the byline.

That feel carried at least a small sense of admiration.

There was not one, but two Arizona newspapers for which Deanne Mulhenney had written. She'd first reported for *The Arizona Tribune* based in Phoenix, and then, somewhat abruptly, she disappeared from the pages of that paper only to reappear in the much smaller *Tucson Gazette*. A fall from grace; apparently the woman's pointed coverage of abuse in the Catholic Church had eventually required her removal from the Tribune, a face-saving move for the paper no doubt.

The woman was dogged and determined. Instead of folding, she'd doubled down with hard-nosed coverage of this year's Arizona senatorial race, and candidate Todd Worwick in particular.

Alena was familiar with that name. Though politics didn't interest her in the least, the business of shaping political outcomes was, quite literally, money in the bank. Before his abrupt departure, Todd Worwick had come from nowhere to be seen, by some, as an alternative to Robert F. Kennedy, an alternative whose politics could be shaped.

Now she saw that it was Deanne Mulhenney who had linked Todd Worwick to a string of unsolved murders in Phoenix...and Los Angeles.

Alena sat back.

"She had help." Chumo, as always, was in perfect sync. He had sat silently at the next machine, spinning through the last two years of news stories from smaller community papers throughout Arizona. Now he moved a photograph from *The Maricopa Sentinel* to the center of his screen.

Alena left her chair for a closer look, gently squeezing Chumo's shoulders as she stood behind him.

The photograph showed Mulhenney and another young woman standing together in the Arizona desert; a dam loomed in the distance. They were consulting with men who wore jackets emblazoned with the words, Maricopa County Crime.

The cut-line read, "MC Medical Examiners collect evidence at Lake Pleasant, assisted by investigative reporter, Deanne Mulhenney and Assistant LA County Medical Examiner, Sara Poole."

Alena smiled.

"She's very pretty," she said.

-=-=-=-=-

There was no bikini in Deanne's ever-ready travel pack. Nor had she thought to include one in her rush to pack and hit the road to cover the assassination of a presidential candidate.

Silly me. Where were my priorities?

A few adjustments to one of Sara's tops – with shorts Deanne wouldn't dare remove covering the bottom of that set, and she was more or less good to go.

Sara, of course, caught male eyes like flies in a pink number that left very little to the imagination.

The so-called June Gloom had graced Hermosa Beach with its absence today and the warm sun, after a quick morning Bloody Mary, followed by Deanne's first ever "ice shot" was the best medicine either of them could have asked for.

The traditional "ice-shot" required the agility, flexibility and general lack of wisdom of the very young. It also required a buddy for support.

The shot's alcohol delivery system was a primitive and potentially deadly sight to behold. Neighbor Bob's system featured an ice-block roughly the height of a full-grown chimpanzee leaning precariously on a tower of cinder-blocks. Various brands and types of alcohol traveled down grooves haphazardly chiseled down its length, chilling said alcohol to frosty, brain-damaging perfection on the way to whoever's mouth happened to be stupidly positioned below.

Since the base of the ice block stood only about three feet above the ground, positioning one's mouth was a limbo-like maneuver that threw any prayer of lady-like behavior to the wind – which, outside of possibly-fatal intoxication, was likely the true purpose of the entire exercise.

Ah...boys...

Sara's laughter, as she "helped" Deanne to shot number 2 was a tonic in itself to Deanne.

Sara squatted before the block, taking Deanne's weight on her thighs and forearms as Deanne leaned backwards.

"Remember, don't inhale!"

The small crowd that had gathered around them counted down.

"One! Two! Three!"

Deanne opened her mouth – and sharp, frigid fluid filled her mouth. She swallowed quickly, coughing as Sara lifted her to her feet.

"Oh my God! I was *not* expecting rum!"

She laughed, half-choking.

"Oh, crud!" Bob, said, standing on the stool above. "That was the vodka hole."

"You're a madman, Bob." Sara chided.

Later, gently baking as they lay in the warm sand, pleasantly intoxicated, their bellies full of barbecued meat, they watched the rolling waves together.

"Do you ever think about him?" Sara said.

There was no question in Deanne's peacefully floating mind which "him" Sara meant. *Tahoma*. He was the real reason Deanne and Sara had met. A Navajo shapeshifter whose name meant "water's edge." A multiple murderer, he had also, oddly, been their protector.

"I do. Sometimes."

Sara leaned back.

"I come out here sometimes...just to see if he'll come walking out of one of those waves..."

"I assume he hasn't?"

"Not yet."

"Maybe he doesn't like salt water."

Sara laughed.

"I am so screwed up, Deanne."

Deanne's hand found hers.

"I think we all are, Sara. But this is nice, isn't it?"

Sara smiled at her, then she looked back out at the waves.

"Yes. Yes it really is."

-=-.=-.=-.=-

Deanne had followed the black cat down a long, dark alley. The cat was gone now, or invisible; one more shadow among shadows cast from a silver moon.

She stood alone at the back staircase of a business she didn't know.

No. Not alone. He's right here.

Purring softly, his wide silver-blue eyes glowed from the rail beside her. She reached to pet him and he smiled up at her.

A Cheshire grin full of vampire teeth -

Deanne woke to Sara's purr-like snoring, her friend lay next to her in the bed, Deanne's arm lay across her friend's tummy. Waves rolled gently beyond the open window.

Deanne had no idea how either of them had come to be here.

She sighed.

She kissed Sara lightly on the cheek and Sara's eyes opened. Sara smiled, drunkenly

"This is nice..." Sara said. "It could be even nicer."

Sara pulled herself on top of Deanne. Deanne froze.

"No...let's not...do this."

Sara rolled her hips slowly into hers.

"Sara!"

Deanne felt Sara's hand slide up between her thighs.

Deanne groaned, *"Sara!"*

"You know this feels good..." Sara purred.

She caught Sara's wrist, gripped it so hard her own knuckles cracked. Even at that, the power she felt in Sara's forearm was terrifying.

"STOP NOW! I MEAN IT!"

Sara blinked. She sat straight up, a look of absolute horror on her face. "I..."

She closed her eyes.

"God, I'm gonna be sick -"

Sara vaulted off the bed. Deanne wasn't sure if she reached the toilet before she retched. The toilet flushed.

Deanne pulled herself up the headboard, breathing hard.

What had she done? She knew how Sara felt about her. What the hell was she doing in Sara's home, in Sara's bed? This was her fault, not Sara's.

Water ran in the sink, then the shower.

Deanne's hotel room was vacant and waiting for her. She could pack the few items she'd brought to Sara's in a minute; should pack them.

But she didn't. The shower turned off.

"Sara?"

She covered herself with Sara's robe and walked into the bathroom.

Sara stood at the sink glaring at herself in the mirror.

"I've turned into my diving coach. *I'm exactly what he was.*"

"You're nothing like him. You were a child; he was a monster. When I asked you to stop, you stopped. That's who you are."

Sara shook her head slowly.

Deanne hugged her tight. She could feel Sara breaking beneath her, their tears met on her cheek. Under her breath she said, "You put on the brakes. I couldn't have done that – you're too fucking strong."

"I love you, Deanne."

"I know you do. I love you too."

"Are you...gonna go to the hotel?"

"Is that what you want?"

"No."

"Then I'm not going anywhere."

-=-=-=-=-

Deanne's sleep was thankfully dreamless this time and when she woke to the rising sun, still in Sara's bed, she was alone.

The emptiness inside the little house was palpable.

"Sara?"

Deanne felt certain she wouldn't find Sara on the couch even before she left the bedroom, but seeing the empty pull-out frightened her just the same.

There's no need to panic.

She'd find Sara walking along the beach, walking it all off. Last night was hard on both of them, but they'd recover. Sure they would.

She pulled on a pair of shorts and a T-shirt and stepped out into the little garden, the odors of last night's barbecue mixed with marine life and overstimulated humanity was heavy in the air.

Last night had apparently been hard on a lot of people.

A few hadn't quite made it back to their homes. They lay snoring in the sand, seagulls picking at the best of the morsels still lying in paper plates nearby.

Miraculously, the ice-blocks were still more or less standing though they'd taken on the eroded look of ancient sculpture; the Hermosa Beach version of Stonehenge.

Deanne walked the beach down to the pier and beyond, then she turned back north toward Manhattan Beach, trying to tamp down a rising fear inside.

Sara was nowhere to be seen.

Chapter 15

B y the time Deanne turned back down the pathway to the house, the bodies had risen, and the Sunday cleanup had begun, if somewhat lazily.

Neighbor Bob had apparently enlisted two young female *recruits* last night. He waved and winked to Deanne as the three of them slowly toppled the ice-block, cheering halfheartedly as it exploded across the sandy grass below.

Deanne practically vaulted the short fence when she realized the music she heard was coming from Sara's bungalow.

She nearly threw open the door.

Sara looked quickly up from her couch. She put down the LA Times and took a deep breath.

"We've got to talk about this."

Deanne nodded, a sickening dread gripped her chest.

Sara held up the paper.

"The polka dots – this is huge!"

Deanne was stunned, happily so. But stunned nevertheless.

"Let's get some breakfast," Sara said.

Mascara. Deanne hadn't missed it, and even as they walked the gorgeous beach toward the pier, she couldn't quite ignore it. At some point after they had come to...an understanding last night, Sara had left, not for a walk, not to clear her head.

Along with the eyeliner...a scent of unfamiliar perfume drifted from her skin.

She'd gone out and met someone. In the condition she'd been in, it was so *irresponsible*. So dangerous.

You're not her mother, you're not her lover.

There are things you will never know about Sara.

And that's just how it's going to be.

And still...

"I'm assuming it was Rick who told you about the polka dot dress."

Sara's voice brought Deanne out of her mental fog. They stood in front of a breakfast diner. Deanne had seen it on her search for Sara this morning, just as the lights had come on. It was partially open to the beach, the rest was mostly windows. Inviting...but at that hour...lonely.

It was anything but lonely now.

Locals and tourists had filtered in, coffee had been brewed, eggs and bacon were frying. Good-natured jabs were traded between the regulars and staff, along with sports talk.

"Outside okay? I can really use the fresh air."

Deanne was just about to suggest it. She nodded and Sara shushed away a seagull from a table not far from the entrance.

"Morning, Sara." A tall, Clarol black-haired waitress smiled brightly as she placed coffee and ice-water – along with a glass of orange juice for Sara.

"Morning, Janice. This is Deanne – she'll need a quick look."

"Pleased," she smiled handing Deanne a one-page menu she'd pulled from her apron.

"Your usual, hon?"

"You know it."

Sara gulped the water. Then she nearly finished the coffee in one long draught, and drank half her orange juice.

She caught her breath.

"Okay. I read your article. What are you holding back about the girl in the polka dots?"

"If she exists, she's more than a witness. A few people said she seemed to be with Sirhan Sirhan. Not talking to him, necessarily, but standing very close. One said a girl in polka dots was screaming, 'we shot him!' just after it happened."

"Oh, my God." Sara shook her head.

"What?"

Deanne glanced quickly down at the menu when she noticed Janice approaching. She refilled Sara's coffee and replaced her glass of ice water.

"I'll go with the corned-beef hash and egg."

"Sunny-side, up?"

"Perfect."

"Toast?"

"Uh...sourdough. And strawberry jam."

"There on the table, hon."

"Oh, yes. Thank you."

"Be right up."

Sara managed a smile for the waitress, but as soon as the woman turned back toward the kitchen she looked like she might explode.

"We had her photo, fabric from her dress! *We could have stopped them!*"

"What are you talking about?"

"I autopsied her grandmother while Kennedy was dying. The woman was murdered the morning before they shot him."

"How can you know that? They don't even know who the girl is."

Sara seemed lost in her own conversation. She sat, silently, going over it all until the pieces came together.

"That's why they were killed. They were there to ID the assassins. I knew it was a hit...I just didn't know... God, Deanne, there was even a bite-mark!"

"Slow down. I've got to catch up."

"Deanne. Our murders. The assassination. They're all connected."

Whatever hangover Sara might have felt had completely lost its grip. Once again Deanne found herself a passenger on a morning drive, but she wasn't a dreamy sightseer on this one – and Mr. Toad from the wild Disneyland attraction was at the wheel.

Between choking down breakfast and a gut-busting sprint to Sara's car, Deanne had heard enough about burnt corpses and autopsies to never eat breakfast – or barbecue – ever again.

But from what Sara had described, it made sense the two bodies recovered from that burning car were connected to the assassination.

John and Jane Doe. John, obviously military or ex-military, and Jane, a grandmother carrying hidden information meant to identify an assassin or accomplice: even if it was her own granddaughter. John was there to protect the woman and deliver her to the authorities.

But someone else delivered them both to Sara before that could happen.

"I've got to look at all of it again – especially the mark on John Doe's hand – I have to compare the radius of that wound to the ones on the other bodies, and the toxicology."

Sara took a blind left turn that nearly tossed Deanne's breakfast straight out the passenger window.

"You can only do that if you're alive!"

"Sorry."

"If they match, our killer was part of the assassination too." Deanne said.

"Yes. The bite on John Doe's hand, if that's what it is, connects them all."

Palm trees, jacarandas and stucco had given way to concrete, steel, and glass. Above it all, the big white Hollywood sign. Somewhere out there, in that massive labyrinth, a multiple murderer was silently stalking another victim.

A female killer. An extraordinary one, with very powerful connections.

"You really think she's a vampire? She bites them for blood?"

"Partly. She likes blood, but she's likely built up reserves and finds other ways to satisfy her need. Raw meat, for instance. She knows what she has. Obviously, she's treating it with hydroxychloroquine. But it's more than that for her."

"The feel of biting? The damage it does to the victim?"

"The visceral, very personal shock of it, certainly. She's obviously trained very hard with knives and who-knows-what else. She's a professional killer – you wouldn't expect her to lead with a bite."

"She's not exactly cold-blooded then."

"No. She's angry as hell. She's in it for the experience of killing, the thrill. The power over life and death."

"Okay...so this comes completely from outer space – but the power over life and death makes me think of something else. You said the gene is a mutation and her parents were likely exposed to high levels of radiation. But it can be dormant and still passed down, right?"

"Yes."

"Do women with full-blown porphyria give birth?"

"I wasn't thinking that angle, but I'll look into it. It does seem pregnancy under those conditions could be dangerous if not impossible. The mother would certainly require special care. But the radiation itself could make pregnancy impossible for a whole host of reasons unrelated to porphyria. If she's barren, that could make her desire for the power over life and death very personal."

Deanne nodded. Bit by bit, the picture of this young, deadly woman was coming together.

"She's obviously attractive. Her victims have all been male. I'm guessing she's attracted to men. In most of these cases she seems to enjoy pleasing them as much as killing them."

"Not hard to understand," Sara mumbled. "But I wouldn't make too much of that yet. Kennedy went after the Mafia hard as Attorney General. Our killer's tied to the mob, either a member or paid to kill for it, which is odd in itself. Mob dirty-work is usually carried out by males."

"Morton and Maharis weren't mob-connected."

"Not that we know of...they still *could* be. And she's killed in Sinaloa, she's international, who knows how many bodies are out there around the world and what gender they are?"

"God, what the hell have we gotten into?"

"We're in way over our heads – but it's not the first time."

"No. But...that doesn't make it any less frightening. Just the opposite."

Deanne took a deep breath. Somehow, they had arrived at the Los Angeles County Crime Lab alive.

Sara pulled into her usual space and parked.

"I could be a while. Do you want to come in?"

"This morning? Not even a little bit."

"No problem."

But as it turned out, Sara didn't take long at all. When she came out, her face was ashen, her shoulders stooped.

"It's gone. The bodies, the evidence – even my notes. *The Feds fucked us again.*"

145

-=-=-=-=-

"Cromwell called the hotel."

Sara lay on her back on a tie-dyed towel she'd spread just beyond the umbrella's shadow. She looked up at Deanne through dark glasses, and nodded.

They'd pitched the old beach umbrella at Deanne's insistence. Finding it had taken digging through the cache of "stuff" left by the owner of Sara's bungalow. The smell of mothballs only barely outfought the odor of mold. But it did provide shade.

"The sun is our friend," Sara had said.

"You never said that in Phoenix."

"Completely different. Here you *lie under* it — there you *walk into* it."

"You'll thank me when you're thirty."

"You're not even thirty."

"And I don't want my skin to get there first."

And that's how it had gone. Just chatter. Nonsense. After the roller-coaster they'd ridden this weekend, nonsensical chatter was what they needed most right now.

Deanne had brought a Thermos down from Sara's bungalow filled with her own special mix of everything else they might need. She half-filled a Dixie cup and handed it to Sara.

"Hair of the dog."

"If I throw this up — it's on you. Literally."

"Face the other way."

Deanne pulled her towel out from under the shadow and sat next to her friend.

"Now that thing looks really stupid and lonely," Sara said, shaking her head at the stained and faded beach umbrella. She added the somewhat derogatory term for Arizona tourists, *"Zonie."*

"Snowbird," Deanne countered.

Sara sighed.

"Keep telling you, that doesn't work west of Arizona."

Deanne considered that as they tipped their cups.

"Alaska's west."

"This ain't Alaska."

"To Zonies and Snowbirds."

Sara swallowed it in one gulp, she shuddered.

"Well, that went down better than expected," she said.

"So what now?" Deanne tucked her legs to her chest and watched the waves.

"Now? I think your call to do 'fuck-all' the rest of the day was a good one. I've had it with deep thought."

"I should call him back."

Sara re-filled Deanne's cup.

"You obviously need more of your 'joy juice.'"

Deanne drank up.

A breeze rose up with the next wave, its soft kiss on her shoulders was pure bliss.

Deanne resisted the urge to say it was "nice." Nice had flipped badly on both of them yesterday. And yet, here they were...heading more or less in the same direction.

"Stop it." Sara said.

"What?"

"Thinking."

Deanne took a long, deep breath of salty air tinged with fruit and alcohol. She flopped on her belly and closed her eyes to the warming sun, and listened to the sweet lullaby of seagulls and gently rolling waves.

Chapter 16

Deanne met Cromwell in Rancho Park, not far from the West LA diner where they'd met on Friday. Thank God, there were lots of leafy trees; Deanne's skin was on fire.

As they walked, she detailed as best she could the similarities between the Morton murder and the Sinaloa hit – including the presence of what appeared to be bite marks on all of the victims – including Maharis and the two found after the fiery crash outside of Griffith Park. Lastly, she'd given the best second-hand descriptions she could muster of the evidence Sara had pulled from the old woman's coat.

Describing forensic evidence without Sara made Deanne feel like a one-armed sculptor.

"We believe it's the same killer – a professional. Very well connected. There's no way we can take someone like that down ourselves. If we can tie those murders to the assassination, the FBI can't sit on it. But we need those notes and photos back if we're going to prove it. We need LAPD's help."

"Kennedy wasn't PD's call from the beginning, Deanne. You knew that the first time we talked."

"You asked me to help you find an accomplice. We've got solid leads – and now you're not interested?"

"I didn't say that."

"It's political."

"Damn right it is. You, of all people, should know how that works."

"Really. What do you know about me?"

"I know you don't protect your sources so well."

"That was..."

MANTIS

"Bad timing. Yeah." The deep lines of his brow showed there had been something so much more than bad timing in seeing her with Sara.

"I'm pulling your chain a little on that," he said, "The truth is, you were right about Malibu. Should have been a priority."

"That was Sara."

"I know it was. Look, it's not like I doubted you before. But knowing Sara Poole's working with you...that woman does not suffer fools."

Prepared to defend her friend, Deanne was suddenly speechless. Whatever response she'd expected from Cromwell concerning Sara, it wasn't that one.

"I also know that, for someone from Arizona, you don't handle the sun so good." He smiled. "Enjoy the beach this weekend?"

"Yes. I did. A little too much."

Her bra straps felt like bands of sandpaper on her shoulders. Her face and back radiated heat. She should never have crawled out from under that umbrella.

He guided her toward a well-shaded bench.

"Welcome to my new office."

It felt good to sit. The tops of her feet were burnt and swelled. Her shoes were killing her. What the hell was wrong with her yesterday? She knew better.

"I'm not saying I wasn't curious before, but I looked a little deeper when I saw you with Sara. Not long ago you took down a big-shot candidate. You got some praise for that, you got your old job back – covering Cub Scout cookouts and bake sales – the local beat. Before that – you went after the Catholic Church. Jesus, you know how to pick 'em. You got a pat on the back for that too – but really, that's how you lost your job in the first place. If anyone should know how all this works – it's you."

She almost blurted out that her investigation of the Chief Medical Examiner for Maricopa County wasn't exactly cookouts and bake sales, but even that seemed minor league now. Cromwell was right. Portnoy had brought her back to the biggest paper in the state – but he'd undercut her every time she'd cast for bigger fish.

It was awful to think of it this way – but if the assassination hadn't happened, if she hadn't been there at exactly the right moment, hit Portnoy with just the right pitch, she wouldn't be here. And once this story was in the books, where would she be then?

"Yeah, I know politics. I know being right doesn't mean rainbows and butterflies. You can win and still lose. So where are you going with this, Rick? Are you telling me you're done?"

He shook his head.

"No. Not even a little bit. Evidence destroyed or sealed, investigation pushed to a new jurisdiction? I'm sick of it too. You might have noticed I've taken a few punches in my life too."

His grin was surprisingly boyish, even impish, despite the scars, the deep grooves in his forehead.

"It's their game, but that doesn't mean we have to play it their way."

Once again, Deanne had braced for the wrong turn on this ride. She considered just what he meant.

"So how far off your beat are you willing to go?"

"Depends what we find. Bottom line for me is we have unsolved murders that don't have to stay that way. Are they all connected? I'm not convinced yet. For now, let's just say I'll take some things on faith I normally wouldn't – and leave it at that."

She'd barely closed the door behind her when Cromwell tapped on her window. He pulled something from his jacket as she rolled that window down.

"I almost forgot this. Nice picture, by the way."

He handed her a photo from a news clipping. The photo was taken just below the Waddell Dam at Lake Pleasant the day after all Hell had broken loose with the Lily Murder case: Deanne and Sara with Sara's new medical examiner friends in Arizona.

"The Tribune agreed not to print this."

"The Tribune didn't. But it did get printed. Some Podunk paper north of Phoenix. Just thought you should know it's out there."

-=-=-=-=-

A quick check in for messages at the hotel and then Deanne was driving her Starfire back to Sara's with the top up for shade but the windows open and the air-conditioner blasting, singing along with Jim Morrison.

The conversation with Cromwell had left her both exhausted and exhilarated. The man was a carnival ride.

She wondered just how hard she could push to stay here a while longer. Portnoy hadn't called her back just yet – but that was coming. Less than a week after the assassination, and already all eyes were turning toward the upcoming Democratic Convention, which was likely to be a full-on brawl.

She'd only been officially back at the Tribune a matter of weeks. Asking for time off was likely a career-limiting move.

Her thoughts turned toward the photo with Sara at Lake Pleasant. It had been mostly staged, and completely ill-advised. Chalk it up to the euphoria of not just solving a multiple murder case – but surviving it.

Not that Deanne minded the publicity, but the appearance of "going rogue" could have ended Sara's career at LA County; she hadn't been in Phoenix in any official capacity. As it turned out, that investigation had been good and bad for Sara, just as it had been for Deanne.

Lost in her thoughts, Deanne didn't notice the deep green sedan following several cars behind her...at first. By the time her own silent alarm went off ten miles closer to Hermosa Beach, the car was gone.

Nothing. She was being paranoid.

She took a deep, calming breath anyway.

No one knows you're here.

-=-=-=-=-

Deanne drove her Starfire under a silver moon with the top down. The wind felt good in her hair, cooled the fire in her cheeks and forehead. Waves crashed in the distance. She was driving up a steep hill between stones piled high as her shoulders; past worn headstones, stone angels and decayed wooden crosses, straight into the black maw of the tunnel ahead.

Blackness.

Driving fast. Driving blind!

But she couldn't stop.

In the mirror she saw nothing but the silver moon chasing her, approaching fast, growing fast.

Something glinted just below it. Deanne snatched the object from her dashboard. She held a bullet in her hand. A high caliber round, full-metal jacket.

Her mirror shattered.

"Deanne!"

Sara ran to her bedroom. Deanne sat against the headboard, eyes wide open. The entire bed shuddered beneath her.

Sara wrapped her arms around her, "You're okay. You're okay. Just a dream."

She doesn't see me.

Deanne's eyes closed. Sara held her until the shaking stopped.

She moved her slowly away from the board, and placed a pillow behind her.

Sara slid beside her underneath the sheet, rested her head in Deanne's lap.

Sara knew all about nightmares. She'd had plenty of her own, and Deanne had called several times in the middle of the night to describe hers once Sara left Phoenix.

This was the first real time they'd spent together since then. The first time they'd been together when the dream came.

What set it off tonight, my friend?

Eventually their breathing synchronized. Deanne was back in a deep, peaceful sleep.

It felt good, so good to have her here, to hold her.

Too good.

Despite her good intentions. Sara couldn't stop her own feelings.

As quietly and carefully as she could, Sara extricated herself from the bedding.

This is hard.

She went into the small kitchen, watched the moon through her gauzy curtains, and drank a tall glass of water.

Today had been hard too. She'd partied way too much this weekend. Been through too much. Seeing Rick was tough after what she'd done. Finding her own work ripped out from under her, once again, was agonizing.

Going to work, going through the motions, going through a typical Monday as though none of those things had happened was a special kind of Hell.

She should have gone to the Dojo tonight, beaten and sweated the sin of alcohol and her frustration out. She'd intended to do just that.

But she hadn't. She'd come straight home.

She and Deanne had shared a quiet dinner in, and that had been nice.

She loved having Deanne in her home. Well, fuck...you love her.

But, once again...it was hard.

Deanne's conversation with Rick was good. One way or another they'd be working together. The truth was, they needed him, and they all needed to be on the same page. No matter how shitty that felt.

No. Fuck it. What had she told Deanne? *Stop thinking.*

She needed, desperately, to take her own advice.

Quietly, she put on her makeup, dressed, and collected her keys and purse.

The Fairfax District and P-Willows were a long way from home. Lately the short drive to Loosies, despite her recent experience with that club and Rick, had become her late-night destination of choice.

In truth, Loosies generally offered a younger, hipper crowd; less show and more discretion.

On the other hand, as she chose a dark booth with a full view of the bar and stage, she realized she'd returned to the scenes of her dates with Rick almost immediately after that disastrous affair, like a criminal reliving her crime.

Let's face it. *You invited him in.*

Once again, stop thinking.

She ordered a Manhattan from a brunette waitress named, of course, Lucy, in keeping with club rules, whose actual name, Sara knew, was Cindy.

Not much going on tonight. Well, it was Monday after all.

The young woman singing LA Woman under the smoke-filled stage light wasn't doing a half-bad job. The clientele was mostly male. A few giggly girl "couples" collecting drinks from the older guys.

One sad, fat, balding little man sat way back in the shadows.

She amended her earlier thoughts about a hipper crowd. Of course, once again, this was Monday night.

She had come, she'd checked it out. All she had really needed tonight was to get out of the house for a little while; exercise her independence from love and work.

When her drink arrived, she almost dropped a tip and left.

Instead, she drank it straight down. It shouldn't have felt as good as it did, not after this weekend.

Through the wavy film of vermouth and bourbon, the woman's red hair nearly matched the cherry at the bottom of Sara's glass.

Sara bit the cherry. She set the empty glass down and ordered another as she watched the shapely young red-head take a seat at the far end of the bar.

All eyes seemed to have suddenly shifted in the redhead's direction. *That one won't be buying her own drinks tonight,* Sara silently mused.

Don't even try, she was thinking, somewhat meanly of the fat little man she'd seen in the darkness earlier. He'd been sitting not far from the seat the woman had chosen. Nowhere to be seen now, he'd obviously given up for the night.

Sara watched as the woman casually ordered a drink, artfully feigning surprise when the bartender nodded to a thick-necked "dude" sitting halfway down the bar before setting the drink down.

As the woman reached for that drink, her long fingers touched the pretty bartender's hand ever-so-lightly, the bartender smiled back.

It was only a moment, it was subtle. But Sara noticed.

Sara sipped down the last of her second Manhattan, feeling the buzz now, and the beginnings of something more than that, a genuine thrill. Sara hadn't really cared to define a "type," though, upon reflection for whatever reason lately her lovers tended toward a softer, fuller look. The redhead was roughly Sara's height. Full breasted, narrow-hipped though not unnaturally so – her long legs and arms were tuned and toned, her belly, what there was of one, completely flat.

She was more than simply attractive, she was gorgeous.

Sara knew the effect she had on others, male and female alike, and in an odd way, she wondered without even a trace of ego, if *this* was, in any way, what they saw in her.

The thick-necked "dude" left the pack and started brazenly toward the redhead.

Sara smiled. This could be interesting.

He'd barely taken two steps before the woman waved directly at Sara. Quickly gathering her purse and the drink, she headed Sara's way.

"Shirley!" the woman called to Sara. As she passed the flabbergasted man, she gushed an emphatic, "Thank you for this!" and finished her happy beeline to Sara's booth.

Sara jumped up to greet her brand new long lost friend.

"I...can't believe it's you...Joan!" She said.

They hugged as if it had been years, *years* I tell you, since they'd last met.

"Thank you for saving me," the newly-christened Joan whispered in her ear. *"Is he still there?"*

"Floating in place," Sara described for her. "Stunned...now he's considering his chances of taking us both home tonight."

"God, I'm so stupid," Joan said. "Please excuse me. I'm going to do something crazy."

She kissed Sara full on the lips with the sweetness of strawberries. Her tongue lightly touched Sara's before she whispered,

"Did that do it?"

Sara almost asked, *"for him...or for me?"*

She swallowed.

Behind Joan, the man's hot and hungry look had soured to something between disappointment and revulsion. He walked, uncertainly, back to the bar.

"He got the message."

"Thank God. I should know better."

Joan slipped into the booth next to Sara. Close...but carefully outside her personal space.

"Yeah, those *free* drinks really aren't...so much."

"No," Joan practically giggled, and it was...cute. Unexpected. So was the feel of Joan's hand on Sara's thigh. There and gone in a moment, but the touch left an invisible warm imprint there.

"Thank you, again." Joan glanced back at the bar, where the beefy boy had already ordered more drinks, likely hoping for better luck with the even younger chippies.

"I've got to go." Joan quickly finished Mr. Beefy's drink, slid her shapely legs out of the booth, and smoothed the thin dress over her perfectly round bottom as she turned to go.

"I was supposed to meet someone here. I'm late. He's probably back at his house by now."

She turned suddenly back and leaned straight over the table to peck Sara's cheek. The low neckline of her dress left Sara no reason to wonder if Joan's breasts were as perfect as the rest of the package. They were.

"I didn't mean to intrude, you've been a sport! But I'm sure you have friends coming."

"I..." Sara started, but she had to catch her breath. "...don't really."

"And sorry about the *Shirley!*" Joan went on. "You don't look like a Shirley. It was just the first name I thought of." She put her hands to her face, "I mean, oh God, that's not your name, is it! I mean, if it is, I didn't mean there's anything wrong with it!"

Sara laughed. The woman was guileless. Sara almost introduced herself as Traci, her standby in similar situations. Somehow, it just didn't seem right tonight.

"Sara. I'm not sure *Joan* quite fits you either."

"I kind of like *Joan.*" The redhead smiled, but I'm Helena. I know...sounds old-fashioned and stodgy -"

"Not at all."

Helena put her hand out this time. An unexpected strength there as Sara squeezed those well-manicured, elegant fingers; the calluses had been pumiced and softened, but they were there nevertheless. This body had not come without careful maintenance and hard work.

"Really good to meet you, Sara."

"Likewise."

A sense of very real disappointment and mystery as the woman walked away.

Have I just been seduced? Is this what it feels like?

And just when she was thinking how sad it would be to never see this woman again, Helena turned back with a completely new thought.

"Oh hey. I'm going to be here for a couple weeks. The guy I'm meeting – I'll be house-sitting for him just a few blocks from here. Do you come in here a lot?"

"I have been, yeah. Maybe I'll see you."

"Hope so!" Helena glanced over at the bar where the chippies had surrounded the beefy free-drink machine. She rolled her eyes, and took a deep breath.

"Thanks again, Sara, for saving my life."

Chapter 17

"Someone's in a good mood today."

Ben shut off the bone saw. Spattered with blood and bone from waist to surgical cap, protective glasses dripping, Sara wondered how that phrase would look plastered over a huge photo of Ben at this moment.

She nearly giggled. Jesus, she *never* giggled.

"Wow!" He said, "Did you beat up a football team last night?"

She shook her head. Even *that* seemed funny.

"No. Just...you know, my friend's in town."

"Yeah, about that – wouldn't mind meeting the famous Miss Mulhenney one of these days."

"You think she's your type?"

"All women are. Present company excluded, of course."

She helped him lift the rib cage from their latest customer.

"Careful with the hinged one."

She nodded. The man before them had died in his office an hour after what should have been a minor traffic incident; little more than slamming on his brakes.

Unfortunately, he wasn't wearing his seat belt. He and his steering column had an unplanned and unpleasant meeting. One rib was broken and hanging, hinged. She'd dissect his heart and lungs in due course, but the amount of blood and other fluids in his chest cavity gave her a pretty good idea of what she'd find there. Heart failure. He likely hadn't died from the damage to his chest, per se, but from the buildup of fluids inside it, the pressure was too much for his heart.

She quickly thumbed through the report.

"He exchanged a few words with the kid he'd almost hit in the crosswalk. Then he got back in his car and just kept driving to work. When he got there he complained of difficulty breathing, intense chest pain."

"Yeah." Ben said. "Five bucks says if he'd gone to emergency instead of work, had those fluids drained, he wouldn't be here."

She shook her head.

"Probably didn't want to make his morning any worse than it already was."

"Now *there's* irony for you," Ben said. "I'm serious about your friend though. Not talking about a date. It's just...I mean I worked on two of those Lily autopsies; Maharis and those crispy critters too."

Now she got it. Sure, Sara had done the extra leg work – even used her vacation time to solve the Lily murders with Deanne. But Ben was her partner too – she didn't do all those autopsies alone. And the FBI's pulling of evidence they'd both worked so hard to collect and identify affected them all.

"You're right, you two should talk; we all should. I'll figure something out."

By lunch time Sara's, humor and spirits were in high gear.

Chances were good she'd never see Helena again, she knew that on some level. But, maybe it wasn't Helena so much as knowing it was still possible to meet someone, someone who could stir things up a little.

But it wasn't the mysterious and somewhat goofy redhead she was girding herself to deal with now. Somehow, she had to thaw the glacier she'd built between herself and Rick Cromwell.

She got as far as the phone.

Her chest felt heavy. Her hand hovered over the dial.

This is nuts. Just dial, call him.

"Sara."

She nearly jumped out of her skin. It was Tim Reynolds from Toxicology, standing way too close.

"Jesus!"

"Are you okay?"

"Yeah, sorry. Just...what's up?"

"Um. You have results waiting." He spoke softly, almost a whisper. *"Like before."*

Sara's heart sped, understanding fully now, just what he meant.

159

"You're right. I do."
"Come by the window at 1:15, they'll be ready then."
"Yes. Thank you for reminding me."

One-fifteen was break time for Merl Boggs. As he carried his bulk around the corner toward the break room, Sara stepped up to the window, folder of bogus case numbers in hand.

"I'm pretty sure I have these." Tim said.

The second hand on the big clock behind the desk swept by nine seconds and the folder was back in her hands, one page protruding from the corner.

-=-=-=-=-

A wave slapped the pilings beneath the pier just below Deanne's feet, sending spray high into the air. Seagulls cried, as they floated above, the braver ones sidling across the guardrail near the bait buckets, only to be shooed away by the crusty fishermen who'd dropped their lines just past the rolling waves.

She would miss this place.

"You sure you can't push this one more week?" Sara leaned against the rail beside her.

Deanne shook her head.

"Back on the local beat Friday. And that was pushing it."

"We're so close on this."

It broke Deanne's heart. They'd go on, of course, they'd keep working this case until they had their killer – but if they didn't do it in the next couple days, it would be over the phone lines again. She didn't even want to think about how lonely it would be from now on.

From now on...even that sounded lonely. So final.

"The only national story they care about is in Chicago. That doesn't help us – and the Tribune's got it covered anyway."

She saw Rick Cromwell walking their way from Pier Avenue, his jacket flapping in the breeze. So much unfinished business.

"Give us a minute?" Sara asked.

"Sure."

God, she's a trooper. Deanne almost looked back out to the sea where she knew the sun was just beginning to dip and paint the water; leave the two of them to their private moment in a purposely public place. In the end, she watched Sara walk slowly up to him. While she always thought of the statuesque Sara as tall – she was a couple inches taller than Deanne, and certainly carried herself that way – that perspective changed as she approached Cromwell.

He stopped and let her come to him.

Distance and the rolling sea covered their conversation, but even from here, the tension was palpable. At first, the man stood there, defiant but silent, as Sara spoke. Finally, Sara hung her head.

This is not going well, Deanne thought, somewhat angry with her own mixed emotions at that.

Finally, Rick put his arms around Sara; he rested his chin on her shoulder as they hugged.

Deanne did turn and look out to the sea then.

When they made their way to her at the end of the pier, their eyes were red.

"It's one person. One killer," Deanne said, forgoing the usual pleasantries.

"I wanna hear what you have." Rick said. "But, frankly, my hearing's not so good these days. It's a little windy out here."

"Well," Sara said, with a somewhat sad smile, "I happen to know this great little fish and chips place..."

Seated at a tucked-away table in a dark corner of Shanty's with orders of fish and chips on the way and a pitcher of pilsner between them – Rick's call, and likely a good one; this would be a night for clear heads. At least clearer than a round of Manhattans would dictate.

"I'm going to say one thing up front," Sara began. "I have information I'm technically not allowed to have..."

"Technically?" Cromwell sipped his beer.

"I might be able to justify knowing the details I'm going to tell you, but I can't show you anything and still work for LA County."

"That okay with you, Deanne?" Cromwell asked.

"Yes, we're off the record."

"Then we keep it between the three of us, for now," Rick said. "If you can convince me we have enough to push this, I'm with you. But if we end up nailing a killer and we don't have anything new, we're in a very deep pile of it. Being unable to convict will be the least of those problems.

"It's possible we won't have a choice. We may have to use the evidence you have. Do you understand that? We do this, there's no going back."

Across the table, Sara's eyes met Deanne's. There was nothing Deanne could tell her. It was Sara's career, as well as the careers of anyone who'd given her those reports. Not to mention possible Civil Rights violations by all of them. They were all on the hook.

Sara nodded, slow and resolute.

"There's a multiple killer out there. We can stop her."

"Okay then..."

The food arrived. They went silent as it was placed. *Conspirators are we...* Deanne thought, breaking the morbidly solemn picture she had of them with one more befitting their current surroundings; in that picture they were pirates secretly planning their next raid.

It made her smile...inside, at least.

Oddly, it felt good. She and Sara were a solid team, but having Rick with them was a very big plus. A level of official non-official support.

He also offered a badly needed dose of harsh reality for both of them.

Over fish and chips and beer, Sara described exactly what she now had. Today, she'd been given the previously non-existent toxicology reports for the two "crispy critters" whose case had been removed from LA County jurisdiction – the star-crossed informant and the man who was supposed to protect and deliver her. The drug-profile, the deadly mixture of psychoactive drugs and stimulants were present in both corpses – along with metabolized remnants of the porphyria medication, hydroxychloroquine.

"I don't have the photos or the patch of polka dot material. They took all of that. I don't even have my own notes – but I do have those profiles. They match the others, and every victim had been bitten at least once."

"You're gonna have to run the whole 'bitten' thing by me again. Fetish-bitten or Dracula-bitten?"

"She may drink blood. But she isn't a vampire, per se – she's porphyric."

Cromwell looked blankly at Sara.

"It's a medical condition," Deanne filled in.

"Well, even without that – sounds like the toxicology profiles are enough to connect them," Cromwell said. "And the old woman with the photo and the patch from that dress – all of that would connect our killer to the Kennedy assassination. No wonder the FBI wanted it."

"So why cut off their sources in LA?"

"Well, I gotta tell you. The agents I know – they're upstanding guys. At the top? Not so much."

"I don't understand the benefit to them? Why not solve this? Are you saying someone high up in the Fed wanted Kennedy assassinated?"

"No. I'm not ready to go there. To me, this stinks of 'cover your a.' There's a whole lot of face-saving being done since Hoover's handling of Martin Luther King. To me, it sounds like they had a good shot at preventing this one – and they blew it."

"They had a source," Deanne said. "They underestimated just how much danger she was in."

Cromwell nodded. "Now...they'd be very happy if no one even knew she existed."

"Toxicology ties John and Jane Doe with Morton and Maharis," Sara said. "That would take an organization behind our killer and big money. Vincent Romano gets us to the Borrono crime family, so does the hit on DeMalo in New York – but I haven't been able to get toxicology on either of them."

"I can get that," Cromwell said. "DeMalo, though...that's a stretch. From what I've heard, witnesses said the hitman was a guy."

"A slight, darkish young man..." Deanne agreed. "We think our killer's somewhat of a chameleon."

"No time for a bite," Sara said. "The hitman knew exactly where to put that knife. One and done. An expert. Like our killer. And DeMalo was connected to the Borrono family, as was Vincent Romano."

Cromwell raised his eyes to the heavens. Instead of the heavens, they found a weathered wooden female, topless, with gigantic red nipples, hanging in the rafters; presumably an old pirate masthead. Deanne saw it for the first time too. Through all their dark talk of murder...*that* had hung over their heads. She nearly laughed. *They had to find a new place to talk business.*

Clearly sharing her thoughts, Cromwell shook the image from his head. Finally, he leaned in.

"You're asking me to risk my stellar reputation with the force to chase a knife-wielding, vampire chameleon?"

"Pretty good summation," Deanne said. "With Mafia connections."

"Six bodies," Sara looked to Deanne.

Deanne nodded.

"Seven seems to be our lucky number," she said, alluding to their first case together, "but I'd rather we don't get there this time around."

"I'll check with INTERPOL," Cromwell said. "If this woman is half what you say she is – that number is likely to be the tip of the iceberg."

"We know the Borrono family is in the drug trade," Deanne said. "With the Vincent Romano hit, we know they have tentacles reaching to Sinaloa, Mexico – maybe even Cuba. Any reason they wouldn't be in LA?"

Cromwell considered that.

"Street gangs here are getting pretty good at moving drugs themselves. Borrono family would be competition. That being said, they could be a supplier. If they're here, they've been able to cover it so far."

The hand was coming together for Deanne. Bobby Kennedy's work as Attorney General could have made him a target for the Borrono family, but there were still two wildcards at play.

"We know Morton was clean..." she said. "Just trolling bars for a loose hottie that night. Maybe it was simply the wrong bar at the wrong time, but what about Maharis? Was he a drug user?"

"Outside of the profile that killed him, I didn't see anything elicit," Sara said. "Then again, the prescriptions he took would have kept most people high as a kite."

"What about people he worked with?"

"Well, it is Hollywood," Cromwell said. "Someone clamped down fast and tight on that investigation; pulled somebody's strings. The studio maybe. A possible Borrono connection gives me some leverage to pry." His eyes inadvertently caught the female masthead again. He looked quickly away, as though his eyes were singed.

"The hell?" Sara had finally seen it.

"It's about time!" Deanne chortled. They all laughed.

"All right," Cromwell put up his hands. "I'm sorry, but I can't get this bloodsucking, biting thing off my mind. You're telling me this killer actually drinks her victim's blood?"

"In some cases," Sara said. "And she seems to like biting. But I'm starting to think there's a bigger purpose to it."

"More than shock value?" This was new to Deanne.

"Yes. The drug profiles are too consistent not to be pre-measured doses – as if delivered through a hypodermic syringe. But she can't be using a standard syringe as a weapon. Way too clumsy to hide and wield," Sara explained. "Our killer is fast and efficient when she needs to be; her life depends on it. The radius and evenness of the bite-marks suggest a denture of some sort. That denture could be hollow."

Cromwell sat back.

"You're saying she stings with her bite? Like a mosquito?"

"The flow of bruising could indicate injection sites at the bite, yes. An insect's not a bad analogy. It's possible her teeth are her syringe."

"Our lady has a sting," Deanne mused.

Chapter 18

It was a nice house with panoramic windows in a once very nice neighborhood near Culver City; secluded, only a few meters from the hill where Chumo crouched peering out the side window of their van. The lights from that house painted the hillside, and even at this distance, Chumo could hear the thump of bass from music playing inside.

A tiny red light blinked on the cylinder tethered to Chumo's spotter glasses. He put the com unit to his ear.

Alena's voice cut through the music inside, *"Empty nest. No Tony, no mark. He set us up."*

Chumo pressed the talk button as he squinted through the mounted binoculars.

"Copy that. Scanning the block. Hold 10 seconds and you're out…starting now."

"Copy."

He checked his neon watch dial and widened the vision on the binoculars. The second hand had swept barely five seconds when he saw two unfamiliar cars, a sedan followed by a long black limousine coming their way. The headlights went dark as the cars silently rolled to the entrance of the cul-de-sac.

He pressed the talk button.

"Bogies in the street. Get out. Back door."

"Copy."

Fuck Tony.

Chumo checked the suppressor. He re-positioned himself behind the machine gun.

He blew out the windshield of the limo before its brakes had set, it rear-ended the sedan in front just as that car's doors flew open, throwing armed men to the pavement. They scrambled to retrieve their weapons as Chumo strafed them. The back wheels caught one unlucky man, rolling him into a screaming ball as the limo continued to push the lead car down the street. His broken body painted a wide shiny stripe in the street.

Chumo swung the barrel back toward the limo where a small army of street thugs jumped like paratroopers from the wide doors, firing blindly, too frightened to locate the source of quiet hellfire raining down on them. Two of them made it to the house.

Chumo stopped firing. Alena could still be inside.

Fuck.

A moment of unfamiliar panic.

He raked both cars one more time.

"Fuuuuuck...Tony." Gino's eyes were wide as he turned Tony's car down the cul-de-sac.

The car was full of extra muscle tonight. So was the one following them. It shouldn't have been needed. The extra guys were along as a "just in case."

Just in case Miguel Sanchez told Tony to his face that he no longer needed Borrono product, which, lately was the word on the street.

Just in case Tony couldn't convince Miguel it was bad business to deal directly with Sinaloa.

Alena wasn't a "just in case." She was an "either way."

Either way it went tonight, Alena was going to be Miguel's parting gift. In other words – Miguel was out – either way it went. And if things happened to go really, really south – that was the *Aliena's* problem.

That was Tony's idea – one Gino didn't like at all...but loyalty was loyalty, and his was to Tony.

The conversation was going to take place during a nice little party at Miguel's – a few girls, some music, some coke...

But all of that was to have started half an hour ago. That was the plan.

One of the men whistled from the back seat.

Gino knew Tony's whistle, and that wasn't it. Definitely one of the other guys.

As they rolled into the quiet aftermath of mayhem, crushing glass beneath their wheels, Tony was silent.

Doing his best to avoid the blood and bodies – *Tony loved his car, and he loved it shiny and clean* – Gino pulled to a stop.

The muscle drew their guns as they stepped outside into the stink of cordite and fresh blood. They fanned out across the scene.

Gibberish and moaning from the limousine.

Gino and Tony held their guns out front as they approached the bullet-riddled vehicle.

Sitting among the shredded bodies, a young, nicely dressed, blood-spattered young woman, mumbled incoherently, miraculously unhit, as she cradled the body of Miguel Sanchez in her lap.

Tony offered her his hand.

When she turned her eyes up toward him, he put a bullet in her forehead.

Miguel coughed a mist of blood into the air.

"I guess you really don't need us now, asshole."

He dragged Miguel into the street, pulled his signature hammer from his belt, and shattered the dying man's skull.

"Front door's open, boss."

"The *Aliena* in there?"

"Tony, as your friend...please..." Gino was terrified.

"Alive?" Tony brushed by Gino.

The front door was wide open to Hell.

Alena walked toward Tony between the gore-strewn bodies of two men, throats and bellies slit wide open, their entrails strewn over the marble floor. The entire entryway was crimson with fresh blood.

She passed Tony without a word and stopped next to his car. His men backed away.

"Any of you gentleman know how to change a tire?"

She looked into each hard face. They said nothing.

"Too bad."

She pointed toward the car's front tires. They exploded with two bursts of muffled gunfire. The men scattered.

"You goddamn, *bitch!*" Tony screamed.

She slammed a knife into his back tire, flattening it, as she continued walking.

168

MANTIS

"Time to learn," she said.

-=-=-=-=-

"You could have been killed."

"But my Chumo didn't let that happen, did he?"

"I couldn't get them all."

She cocked her chin. She smiled, benignly at her little man.

"It was two men, Chumo. Only two. Three? That might have taken more time."

He shook his head.

"Overconfidence kills."

She softly massaged his neck with one hand. With the other, she held an AK47 rifle across her lap.

"Tony is a bigger problem than I thought," she said. "I'll admit that."

"Your uncle will call for a sit down after this."

She nodded.

"It's due. One way or another the Hammer needs to be brought down." She added, "The office will want to know."

"I'll take care of it."

Alena watched the sandy hillsides pass by, the hills gave way to a wide, flat marsh, beyond that...the Pacific Ocean.

"It may be time to rethink the family's role."

"That's not for us to decide, Alena."

She sighed, as they pulled to a stop next to Alena's green Alpha Romeo.

"Chumo." She looked directly into his eyes. "Are you ever sorry I brought you in?"

"*Always.*" He said. Then he smiled at her and shook his head. "Such a silly question. Never."

She kissed his forehead.

"Are you coming home?" He asked.

She rolled back the door, locking it behind her.

"In the morning," she said through the window. "One or two loose ends to tie before Uncle Toro calls."

He nodded.
"I'll stand by."
Alena shook her head.
"Get some sleep, Chumo. I'll call."

-=-.=-.=-.=-

A quick stop at the still vacant South Bay house to wash the blood away, and the freshly showered and powdered beautiful redhead was roaring toward Manhattan Beach.

Fresh from the kill. Exhilarated and high.

Her showdown with Tony the Hammer had been long in the making, inevitable. The evening's mix of fear and ultimate conquest, the scents of blood, of gunpowder, the thrill of the fight, of taking those men, the utter domination of Tony, had left her thrilled and wanting more.

She'd prepared a few special mixtures tonight. She carried the capsules, the hypodermic dentures in her purse the way old-west American gunslingers carried pre-loaded cylinders for their revolvers.

Rarely indulging in drugs herself, she had, in fact, tasted and tested them all early in her career, coolly and clinically gauging their effect for the most part, but genuinely enjoying the experimentation with some.

Tonight...she'd taken another rare step.

During a slow, post-shower stretch and a demonstration of flexibility that would fill a Yogi with envy, she'd bitten herself high on the inner calf, *tasted her own blood, filled her own veins with fire.*

Sara Poole was more than a *mark*. Alena knew that the moment they'd met.

Reading people, adapting to them, was a talent Alena had learned early on from her mother – the only killer Alena knew to be more efficient and deadly than herself.

Alena had read something in Sara, and with that, felt something extremely rare for Alena. *Actual desire.*

Certainly Sara was a beautiful girl and that was part of the attraction. More than a tinge of jealousy added spice to it. Alena had the power to be beautiful – but not the nature. She knew very well what she was – essentially a perfect mannequin.

Chumo, the only living being other than Alena's parents to see her completely naked, knew exactly what she was. Chumo desired her unconditionally and she loved him for that.

But Sara's beauty was real. And like Chumo, so were her feelings.

She was also somewhat innocent and naive. There was something broken and wanting there, a genuine need.

And that need could be exploited.

Alena passed the little side street where Sara Poole and Deanne Mulhenney shared Sara's bungalow. Were they lovers? If not now, Alena was sure they had been.

This wasn't the first time Alena had visited their little nest. If Sara didn't appear at *Loosies* tonight, Alena would pay one last and very final visit here.

But if she had read the beautiful Sara correctly...the girl waited for her now, flush with her own desire.

-=-.=-.=-.=-

"Sara!"

It was Rick's voice. Deanne rubbed her bruised knee and ankle. She'd slammed both on Sara's nightstand while diving for the phone.

"Rick? It's Deanne."

She stumbled out into the main room.

The pull-out was empty. Sara was gone...to wherever she had been going these late nights.

Deanne's mind raced – she and Sara had celebrated Deanne's last night in LA with dinner and Manhattans, a last walk along the beach together, followed by two more Manhattans -

"She's...out -"

"Where?!"

"I...don't know...exactly."

She heard him take a quick breath. Had he just said, "Dear god?"

"I'm close by." He said. *"Lock the door and stay put until I get there!"*

171

"Where are we going?"

She'd barely dressed by the time Cromwell knocked. And now they were running down the path to his car.

"Loosies. You know the place?"

He practically threw the passenger door open. She slid quickly inside and cinched the seat belt tight. Surely another Mr. Toad's wild ride lay ahead. She felt the door slam shut in her temples.

"It's a bar up the road in Manhattan Beach. Sara had me meet her there...one night. I think that's where she is now and where Morton met his killer."

The horror of that situation finally cut through everything – the fog in her head, her disappointment in Sara's dangerous, self-destructive flings. Now, she was terrified for her.

"Why there?"

"Hunch. Something you threw out the other night got me thinking - that Morton was out looking for a loose hottie. What better place to do that than a bar named Loosies; a pick-up joint you've passed half a dozen times looking at houses."

"You're scaring me. Morton looked at a lot of houses."

Deanne saw the neon flash of the *Loosies* sign just before they careened around a corner, and Cromwell screeched to a stop.

"Yeah. Well, today we found out three of 'em are practically in Sara's backyard. I don't see her car, do you?"

Deanne shook her head.

"She could be anywhere within a mile – she's not afraid to walk -"

"Yeah, I know. She's fearless," he said. "That's the damn problem."

He half-marched, half ran to the door. Deanne could barely keep up.

"Rick. Tell me what's different? What happened today?"

He barely slowed as he opened it and ushered her inside.

"Another body washed up – a woman this time, right off Will Rogers Beach in Santa Monica. Real estate agent. Turns out Morton was high on her client list – we're checking the others out now."

-=-=-=-=-

A red light blinked beneath the dash. Alena popped the glove compartment open, pulled the com device from its holder and pressed the talk button without so much as a glance; her eyes on the rear view mirror and the car following close behind.

"Go ahead."

"You're booked on American, 6 AM to Newark. Ticket will be delivered to the hill house."

She sighed.

"Copy that."

She rolled her window down just enough for the courier's delivery. Waves crashed against the cliffs below as the sea air blew in.

"I can be on that flight too."

"It's my problem, Chumo. I'll take care of it."

She snapped the com back in place and shut the compartment. As she turned onto the horseshoe driveway and parked, Sara's car rolled in right behind hers.

Alena smiled.

Plenty of time.

-=-=-=-=-

Rancho Palos Verdes wasn't an area Sara ventured to often. Only slightly less snooty than Bel Air but prettier, located atop the cliffs that made up the bottom prong of the LA South Bay horseshoe.

Helena was practically giddy. She opened the double doors wide.

"You're going to love this view!" she said.

And who wouldn't. From the entryway Sara could see all the way to the lights of Marina Del Rey through the glass back doors and windows.

Helena opened the patio windows wide and the ocean breeze filled the entry.

"Careful, there's fresh paint everywhere."

The breeze took the usual scents of linseed oil away – but plastic sheeting still lay in the huge den area.

"Wow..." was all Sara could manage. "What does your friend do?"

"He's a trust-fund baby, so as little as possible – not enough to keep this place. Go ahead and sit down, take in the shoreline."

Sara nearly missed the step down to the sunken den.

How the heck did you drive here?

She pulled the plastic covering from the plush sedan and eased herself onto it. The lights of the South Bay twinkled along the coast, the breeze felt so good against her skin. The snap, slide and click of glassware behind her as Helena's reflection in the window opened the long bar at the back wall.

"Let's see...you like bourbon, right?"

"I started that way – but whatever you're having."

"You know, there's some very well-aged Aglianico here – wanna try some?"

"I have...no idea what that is. But, sure."

She took the glass Helena offered.

Helena curled up next to her on the couch, close enough Sara could feel the warmth of her, taste the intoxicating perfume of her skin. She lifted her glass.

"To some of the best scenery in California," Helena toasted. They clinked the balloon glasses. The wine was deep and smooth and wonderful.

"Out there? Or right here...?" Sara asked.

Helena slid one strap of her dress down her shoulder, then the other.

"What do you think?" She purred.

They tasted the wine through their kiss. Her lips were warm and so soft.

They each took a deep, long drought of wine and set their glasses down.

"I think..." Sara said hoarsely, "I'd like to see more..."

She slowly bared Helena's breast and took her pink nipple into her mouth, she sucked softly. Helena pulled her to her, then she drew a long deep breath; she lay back and pulled Sara onto the warm, flatness of her belly.

Sara felt Helena's fingers on the back of her thighs, sliding her dress up to her waist...the warmth of her fingers traveled slowly, surely, then deeply inside her.

-=-.=-.=-.=-

MANTIS

The red light blinked, noiselessly, from the travel bag Alena had dropped next to the front door of the hill house in Rancho Palos Verdes.

Chumo pocketed *his* com device as the car continued toward him down the long driveway to their Mandeville Canyon home. He holstered a Walther PPK beneath his smoking jacket before he opened the front door of the guest house.

Tony's car, with three new mismatched wheels lacking the fancy hubcaps, pulled to a stop in the driveway. Chumo couldn't help a smile.

Tony and Gino stepped out.

"What can I do for you gentlemen?"

Even from here, Chumo could feel the seething heat coming from Tony. The Hammer's jaw was clenched tight.

Gino spoke.

"We're here to make sure Alena gets on that plane."

"That's very kind. But she prefers to park her own car."

"You're a funny little man," Tony took a step forward, and Chumo drew his gun.

The shot kicked Chumo backwards. He heard the pop coming from the road above them a split second after the Walther PPK slipped from his useless hand. He spun and ran for the door. The next shot took out his knee. He dropped painfully onto it and screamed.

Tony kicked him squarely in his shattered leg.

"Two can play that fucking sniper game, asshole."

Two more men jumped from the back of the car; they dragged Chumo roughly up the steps to the main house and broke open the door.

"Gino, check out the little man's playhouse."

"She's not here!"

"I hope you don't mind if we have a look-see."

Tony's hammer struck Chumo's broken shoulder.

He blacked out.

-=-.=-.=-.=-

175

"Yes," the waitress said, handing Cromwell's photo of Sara back to him. "She was just here a little while ago. She left with her friend."

"Did they say where? Another bar?"

"Seemed like they couldn't wait to be alone..." the bartender added. *"If you know what I mean."*

"Her friend mentioned a house," the waitress said.

"Who's her friend?" Deanne asked. "What does she look like?"

"A real doll. Red head. I mean like – dark cherry red. Helen or something."

"Helena," the bartender corrected. "I think she's got a sister, if that helps."

"That blonde?" the waitress asked.

"Yeah."

"Thanks," Cromwell said over his shoulder, half-running to the door with Deanne.

"Oh, God." Deanne's heart sank. "Rick, we've got to find her now!"

Cromwell stuck the cherry to the top of his car. It flashed and the siren split the air as he swung the car around and sped back down Hermosa Avenue.

He called in his position and gave three addresses for backup.

"God!" Deanne's heart pounded.

"Hang on," he said.

The house was a wide ranch style, dark but for one dimly lit room. They screeched to a halt out front.

"Stay put."

"Not a chance."

Cromwell shot her a glance.

"I'm a sitting duck in here anyway. I've got a gun."

She pulled the .38 Special from her purse.

"Of course you do. Stay behind me."

She did do that, following close as he ran up the walk with his gun drawn. He pounded on the front door.

"Police! Open the door now!"

MANTIS

-=-=-=-=-

"Somehow, I didn't think you'd be a wine connoisseur," Sara said, although, even to her it came out slurred, almost unrecognizable.

Helena smiled down at her. Her beautiful pale skin seemed to glow in the moonlight, a pulsing halo that made her look absolutely angelic. Sara was exhausted, exhausted in the best way anyone could be.

How many times had they made love? She had lost count, lost track of everything.

"So...*you think you know me?*" Helena mused.

It was time to leave. Alena had packed her travel bag, and left it in her car before she'd left for Loosies. The trip to New Jersey wouldn't be a long one. She would soothe her uncle, soothe the tension in the family, and Uncle Toro would do to Tony exactly what needed to be done.

But for now, she looked down at Sara with a feeling that was...unfamiliar. The nickname she detested, Aliena, came to mind; the emotion was completely alien to her. She couldn't match it to anything she'd felt before, but as she looked down at the still and perfect young body beneath her, the name of that feeling, its real name came through.

Sorrow.

No time for this.

She reached for the long knife hidden beneath the sedan.

"Shomhaow... didn't think you'd be why'n conshur."

Alena blinked.

"So...*you think you know me?*"

A beautiful angel looked down upon Sara with gossamer, shimmering wings, translucent shimmering skin.

Sara watched her own hand reach out, as if on its own, to touch that skin. A tremor, waves of warmth and light pulsed at the touch. She could hear the light, taste it...

"I know...I'd like to. You're...so beautiful, Helena."

Helena drew a slow deep breath.

Hearing light, tasting light...strange words came to Sara through the fog...synaesthesia...*psychotropic...something...*

Alena had drawn her legs to her chest, just beyond her thigh – Sara's wine glass glowed from the table, pulsing with the sound, the taste, of red...

Psychotropic...drugs.

And there, high on Alena's beautifully sculpted calf...

A bite mark.

Sara's block came from pure, practiced reflex. The knife whickered out of Alena's hand and skittered across Sara's back before it shattered the wine glasses on the table and slid across the floor.

She caught Helena's throat, the woman's knee knocked Sara's hand free before Sara could squeeze. Helena's heel slammed Sara's gut. Sara felt herself flying backwards – she reached out and caught Helena's foot as the woman dove for the knife; they both rolled to the floor.

Helena spun into her; sank her teeth deep into Sara's shoulder. Sara's palm cracked against the woman's temple, and Helena released.

Helena staggered to her feet. A moment's hesitation as she gauged the distance to her knife. She spun back on Sara.

Sara sucked breath. Bright lights flashed all around her. No pain from the bite; the horror of just what that meant – *anesthetic injected along with the full dose of their multiple killer's, Helena's, venom.*

For a moment they looked directly in each other's eyes, and then -

The moment Helena's heel lifted, Sara shot forward, struck two sharp powerful blows to Helena's ribs before Helena's kick even began.

Helena fell to her knees beside the knife, wheezing. She scooped it up somehow, flipping the blade into her hand to throw.

Sara yanked a pillow from the sedan, crouching, she held it out just below her sight line. Lights were blazing, Sara's heart pounded with the explosive force of timpani. She knew she didn't have long to fight, to move...maybe to live.

Even from here, with the bright pulsing light, the pounding of blood in Sara's temples, she saw something odd, very wrong with Helena's eyes.

But for her pupils, the woman's eyes were colorless. The contact lenses she must have worn had fallen out. She wheezed, staring up at Sara, holding the knife cocked and ready to throw. She reached into her mouth with her other hand. Something popped, Helena pulled the denture from her mouth and dropped it to the floor. She reached deep into her hair. Another pop. The deep cherry wig fell beside the denture.

Helena staggered to her feet. For a moment she held her breath and stood completely naked in front of Sara; light pink, hairless...a beautifully perfect and blank slate, a mannequin.

"Now, you know me..."

She turned and lurched out the front door. Moments later, Sara heard the Alpha Romeo rev and pull away.

It was the last thing Sara heard before the timpani inside her head, the thumping in her chest, reached a crescendo.

All was still. Then all went black.

A few minutes, a few miles later, barely able to breathe, her chest aching from the pressure, Alena pulled off the road. She wasn't going to make it to the airport.

The envelope with her ticket lay on the seat beside her where the courier had left it. When she picked it up something slid out.

The courier had left more than her ticket.

A red skirt button, blackened and melted at the edges, lay on the seat; one of the buttons she'd left as breadcrumbs for her first lover, her first victim, to follow. A warning only her mother could have sent.

"You're walking into a trap."

No she wouldn't be going to New Jersey. Not today.

Alena made a quick selection from the belt of colored capsules in the lining of her bag, inserted them into a new denture, and popped them in place.

She coughed out the last short breath she could manage, and without a moment's hesitation, bit herself just above the wrist. She squeezed down.

A terrific jolt and Alena was alert, strong. She pushed open the door, braced herself, and plunged the knife just deep enough into her side, letting the clear fluids mix with her blood, and sluice to the sand.

Minutes later, sewn, patched, dressed, and high as a satellite, Alena Evanova was on the road to Mandeville Canyon.

-=-=-=-=-

The light on Chumo's com remained dark. The shattered device lay on the stones just outside the doorway of the Mandeville guest house where it had fallen.

The one in Alena's hand pulsed blue; connection broken. The unit fell noiselessly from her hand to the seat beside her as she turned up Mandeville Canyon Road.

The raw heat driving her went suddenly cold. The dark trees, the hillside, passed by impossibly slow. Then all was still.

A recalculation, no more than that.

Half a mile from home, she coasted slowly off the road.

-=-=-=-=-

"It's time, boss," Gino said. "Her plane leaves in an hour. She was comin' here first, she'd be here by now."

Two men flanked the stool where Chumo sat, duct-taped in place, blood soaking the cushion beneath him.

Tony the Hammer continued peering between the drapes.

Outside, their backup car rolled up behind his. Three men stepped out. One, armed with a machine gun, stood watch. The other two popped opened his trunk. They began filling beer bottles with gasoline, plugging them with rags. Their driver stayed behind the wheel, the car idled.

Tony shook his head.

"No call from Johnny yet. The Aliena ain't shown at the airport."

"Not like her to be late, Tony."

Tony spat. He stepped up to Chumo.

"This is for my tires, dickhead."

He chunked the claw of his hammer straight through the top of Chumo's skull, blood and matter followed the hammer out. Chumo bleated, then babbled.

"Boss! Jesus."

"I gotta take a leak. Then we go." Tony headed down the hallway.

"Johnny calls, tell him to give the Aliena my love."

The men looked from each other to the dying man as Tony disappeared down the narrow hallway.

Chumo continued to babble.

One of them drew his gun to end it. Gino stopped him.

"Don't do it."

"But...Jesus, Gino..."

"It's Tony's call."

"Where's the fuckin' toilet!" Tony called over his shoulder.

Fuck, who cares?

The Aliena's entire house was his fucking toilet. Tony unzipped his fly. He saw wet, muddy footprints on the carpet below him.

"Fuck I know," Gino answered. The creepy babbling was getting to him now. He nearly pulled his own gun, put an end to it.

A *bang* from outside sent the other men to the window. Gino nearly jumped out of his skin.

"Tell me they didn't light the fucking rags!" Gino said.

"Naw. It's not them," one of the men said. "They're lookin' up the hill. Gotta be Ricky up in the trees."

"The fuck's he doin,' huntin'? Joey, get out there - tell him to put the damn suppressor back on. This ain't the only house on the block."

Joey shook his head. Dutifully, he opened the door and shouted to the men.

"Tell Ricky to use the silencer...the damn suppressor."

Gino's nerves were trip wires. He didn't like being in Alena's house, didn't want any of this – and the awful sounds coming from the grotesque little ball of blood.

Chumo's babbling became a long, rasping gurgle – then a terrible, wet gag –

Gino looked up.

That gag didn't come from Chumo.

Tony's bulky frame staggered from the hallway, his eyes wide open and as red as the spray fanning from his open throat. His fat fingers groped uselessly at his tongue – trying to stuff the twitching meat back up through his gaping wound.

Something struck Tony hard from behind; throwing him to the floor.

Alena's blade wickered over Tony's falling body, it split Gino's forehead before the scream left his throat.

She fired two shots through the man standing, frozen, at the window. He crashed through it and struck the pavement below before he felt the bullets.

And Joey never even saw her second knife coming.

Some thirty minutes earlier, Harry Champlain had woken to the not-so-distant sounds of an argument at Helena's house.

Helena didn't have to tell him something was wrong. Their wide and seemingly endless river of sex had dried up just a few nights ago.

He'd half-expected trouble of one sort or other coming his way.

Harry didn't like to think of himself as a jealous man. Hell, at this point in his life – Helena had made him the luckiest old man in the world. He wasn't stupid. Helena was young. Only a matter of time before she stepped out, and someone else stepped in.

Nah, he wasn't jealous...just damn curious.

Men's voices. He recognized the voice of Helena's odd little friend, Charles – the other two were unfamiliar.

Harry trained his field glasses on his pretty neighbor's house – at least what he could see of it.

What he couldn't see was the front of the house. Not from here.

But he distinctly heard little Charles cry out, and two muffled pops – and those sounds he understood very well.

Anyone else would have grabbed their phone and called the police. Harry Champlain grabbed his hunting gear, and loaded his shotgun.

Harry crouched as headlights raked the trees around him. A car made its way down Helena's driveway where another unfamiliar car was already sitting. Three heavily armed men stepped out, one with a machine gun.

Those fellows are definitely not cops. What the hell have you gotten yourself into, my little dove?

And where had those two shots come from?

Had a six-pointer been grazing in front of Helena's house, Harry knew exactly where *he'd* be standing to bag him.

Harry kept low, moving surely and silently there.

The sniper leaned with his full weight against the tree beside him. One eye closed, the other trained down the scope; he had actually looped the rifle's strap over a branch for support.

Harry stood not six feet from him. The guy was focused, Harry'd give him that.

"Say, is that a thirty-aught-six?" Harry asked.

The man nearly jumped out of his wingtips. He struggled to bring the gun around – the strap stopped him.

"Twelve gauge," Harry said as he blasted him.

He quickly unhooked the dead-man's rifle strap and brought the rifle to his shoulder.

The scope magnified the melee below as the confused men mixing Molotov Cocktails ducked and pointed in his direction, not sure what the hell was going on above them. Mr. Machine gun primed his weapon and Harry crouched low.

The man brought the weapon up. He didn't fire.

But it was the men mixing the cocktails that worried Harry most.

The front door of Helena's house opened – a man shouted something Harry couldn't make out. And then – *chaos.*

Two loud shots flashed inside the house and a body crashed through the front window. The man who'd just stepped outside, dropped to his knees, his body tumbled headlong down the front steps, a knife handle protruding from his back.

The men raised two bottles and lit them.

Harry shot one man square through the shoulder, that bottle exploded against the stone driveway and flames engulfed him.

The other managed to heave his flaming bottle through the shattered front window before Harry shot him dead.

The living room lit brightly, a hellish, jack-o-lantern orange.

"HELENA!"

Machine gun fire erupted sending Harry flat to the ground. Bullets snapped branches, tearing the earth all around him.

The second car swung madly back toward the road as the door swung open – the machine gunner jumped in, strafing the front of the house as the car careened back up the drive.

A loud *"WOOOMF!"* and the gas can exploded.

"HELENA!"

Harry charged down the hill as the car hit the road above him and sped away.

The heat threw Harry backwards before he'd even reached the driveway.

-=-=-=-=-

Alena knelt before Chumo as flames raced across the carpet, over the couch and up the bookshelves. Curling gray leaves of wallpaper ash floated around her. She coughed smoke from her failing lungs.

"Can you hear me, my little man?"

One, bloody eye opened. Chumo's lip curled upwards, a whimper, and then a red tear dripped down his cheek.

"Don't cry my little man. I'm here."

She wrapped her arms around him. The flames roared.

She kissed his lips. She kissed his throat and bit down hard.

Chumo shuddered as her venom filled his veins. He groaned.

"No...no...no, my Chumo. It's time to sleep."

She squeezed his shaking body tight.

As the flaming ceiling began to crumble and fall, she bit him one last time.

-=-.=-.=-.=-

A fury of lights, cops and emergency vehicles surrounded the house. Deanne braced herself as Cromwell slammed on his brakes behind the last squad car and they rushed through the chaos behind Cromwell's raised shield.

The call had come in just as Rick prepared to breach the Manhattan Beach house: They'd found Sara, unconscious, at the house in Palos Verdes.

Attendants lifted the gurney over the threshold. It carried Sara's still form, the oxygen mask fogged with her breath.

Thank God.

But if Rick hadn't called in the other units. If they hadn't found her in time...

"Go with her," Rick said, hoarsely. "I'll be right behind."

-=-.=-.=-.=-

Deanne held Sara's hand as she watched her sleep. It had been a tortuous night, God only knew what Sara had been through. Her fight continued into whatever dreams, whatever psychotic landscape the drugs had taken her.

She was breathing on her own now, sleeping peacefully at last.

There was a light tap on the window behind her.

Deanne nodded to Rick as she folded Sara's hand over the blanket.

She closed the door softly behind her.

"Doc says Sara gave the medic a damn accurate profile of what they'd find in her before she passed out," Cromwell said.

"I think she's got that memorized now."

Cromwell shook his head, watching her through the window.

"She is something else..."

"That and a half," Deanne agreed.

"Thanks to that hellcat in there, we think we've ID'd our multiple murderer. Sara knocked her teeth out. Denture was on the floor next to a wig. Hypodermic – just like Sara figured it would be."

Deanne was stunned. A hard jolt, mixed with admiration and terrible regret Sara had faced that horror alone.

"What's her name?"

"She went by a lot of 'em. Real one seems to be Alena Evanova. Interpol's tried to nail her for years. Chameleon was a good word for her."

"A Russian?"

"By way of Cuba – going back to the glory days; Meyer Lansky, Lucky Luciano, and the Borrono family."

"You said, 'was.' She's dead?"

"A house on that real estate agent's list burned to the ground last night not long after they found Sara. Looks to have been torched. Several bodies – all male so far."

"You're sure this *Alena* was in the house?"

"Still too hot to search, but they found a car down the road with more hypodermic dentures and drugs. Car's registered to the same fake name as the house. It's hers."

Chapter 19

"It's like a war zone," Deanne said as she and Rick made their way down the driveway.

"Pretty much."

The big house had taken most of its guest house along with it when it burned. A lot of trees too. A wooded canyon in the summer? The fact the house hadn't taken the entire Mandeville Canyon with it was a miracle. Deanne had been on a few crime scenes now – at least the burnt trees made this one smell better than the others.

A blasted, burnt out shell of a car sat on its side between the buildings. They'd passed one chalked silhouette in the wooded area near the road. Four more silhouettes were outlined outside the blackened foundation of the house; one on the front steps, another not far from that one, two more behind the car.

Blackened pools of blood stained the steps to the guest residence; a trail of it led to the main house.

Tagged evidence, mostly bullet casings, seemed to be everywhere she looked. A photographer moved carefully between them, cataloging everything as Sara's friends from LA County slowly, meticulously poked through the ashes beyond the yellow tape.

Sara would be spending at least one day in the hospital for observation. Deanne had spent the entire night at her side. Deanne's call to Portnoy at the paper had been surprisingly brief, she was staying put in LA, at least for now.

Two men stood just off the property. The taller of them had bandaged hands. His white hair, eyebrows and what had likely been a thick mustache were singed. His face was reddened and blistered.

"Is that our witness?" she asked.

"Yeah, Harold Champlain," Rick nodded as he walked her over to meet him. "And the neighbor I'd most like to have in a pinch. He's responsible for three of those chalk marks."

"That's not a problem?"

"No," he said. The look Rick gave Deanne said, whether it was or wasn't...it wouldn't be.

"Mr. Champlain, I'd like you to meet a friend of mine. Deanne Mulhenney, Investigative Reporter."

Harry nodded slowly.

"I couldn't get to her..." he said.

Deanne shook her head.

"Alena?"

"Helena," the man corrected. "Her name was Helena."

"Helena. She was your neighbor?"

He nodded slowly, "yeah, she was."

"I'm Prentice, Prentice Perkins," the other man announced. I live two houses down. This...is just terrible. Harry is a hero!"

"Yeah, he is," Rick said. "Those men were mobsters, and heavily armed."

"But...I couldn't save her." Champlain said.

"You're certain she was inside the house at the time?" Deanne asked.

He nodded. "Someone in that house fought back – it wasn't Charles, the man who lived with her. I'm pretty sure that's his blood on those steps in front of the guest house. I heard a couple shots fired before I got to the sniper up there; Charles wouldn't have been in any shape to fight back.

"I saw two flashes inside the house, two gunshots. One man came crashing through that window, another one went down those steps with a knife in him."

"And you think Helena...did that?"

"Miss Mulhenney. I'm a hunter. You ever corner a wild animal, even a small one?"

She hadn't, but she knew what he meant.

"Helena was...wild. I think she fought like Hell. But right now?" He took a breath, clearly holding back tears. "I can't even say what I'm doing is thinking."

One of the medical examiners shouted something from the burnt out house.

"They've found human remains inside," Rick said.

"Oh, God no..." Harry sobbed.

"Um...Detective?" It was Prentice Perkins.

"Yes."

"You should tell your friends to be careful walking in there – there's a basement and tunnels underneath the floor. They go all the way to the creek, if you can call it a creek."

"What?"

"Oh yes. During Prohibition that house was owned by a famous Hollywood director! A Speakeasy, that's what they called them in the day," he said proudly. "The best way to keep your guests out of jail? Give them an escape route."

-=-.=-.=-.=-

Deanne held Sara's forearm as they slowly made their way down the hospital corridor. Sara guided the wheeled IV contraption beside her.

"You're a little open back here."

"See anything you like?" Sara quipped as Deanne pulled the garment tight and retied the strings.

"I prefer my partners slightly more...ambulatory."

Sara coughed. They resumed their progress slowly up the corridor.

"So there were meat lockers in the basement." Sara hadn't been surprised in the least when Deanne had told her of the grisly find. "Full of cuts and other offerings your local butcher doesn't provide."

Deanne nodded. "Including many, many liters of human blood."

"Well, that should keep Ben and all my friends back at County busy for a while."

Sara slowed her already slow pace.

"Man...this sucks."

"You sure you should be walking?"

"I can't stand being in that room. You know the windows don't even open?"

She stopped suddenly. Deanne caught her.

"You know..." Sara's face went pale. "Maybe this wasn't such a great idea. Let's go back."

Deanne nodded.

They made it the short distance back to Sara's room without incident. Deanne helped her back into the bed, untangling the IV as Sara slid beneath the sheet.

"So she stole a car?"

"A car was stolen in Brentwood that night, we don't know for sure she did it."

"That's a hike from where you say her house was. Hard to believe she'd leave her car and her stuff, just to steal another one a mile away."

"Not a bad idea – if she wants us to think she's dead. Something else, there was blood in her car, lots of it. Driver's side. They think it's hers."

"Was it porphyric? I hit her hard, I didn't cut her. It'll take a day or two for the lab..."

"Maybe you should give this a rest."

"That's the weird thing...I can't stop thinking."

"You've been saying some pretty awful things in your sleep."

"You ever had acid?"

"Uh...no."

"Me either...until the other night – along with everything else she gave me. I've forgotten most of the dreams...but...now I know what they mean by a bad trip."

"I can't even imagine." Deanne shook her head, something else she'd been wondering, "Can bodies burn so badly they can't be identified?"

"Well...if they're cremated, but that takes a hell of a lot of heat. Usually they just cook. You open them up – and it's like turkey giblets in there."

"Well...there goes Thanksgiving..."

"You asked. Rick told me Borrono's men tossed Molotov cocktails through her window. An accelerant like gasoline could certainly get a hot fire going...still..."

Sara's lids closed, she drifted.

Deanne pulled the blanket up. Sara's hand found hers and squeezed it softly.

"I want to show you something," Sara murmured. "Kind of an old joke... 'wanna see where the whale bit me, sailor?'" She smiled.

She pulled her garment down past her shoulder. Her fingers worked the tape over the gauze patch, and tugged it open.

A hideous patch of yellow, green and purple flesh surrounded an even uglier ring of perfect semicircular cuts.

The sight of it took Deanne's breath away.

"Just like my customers..." Sara said. Her eyes opened.

"I didn't knock her teeth out, Deanne. I know Rick likes saying that...she took them out. She set them on the floor right in front of me...her wig too. She wanted me to see her as she is. *She wants me to find her...*"

Plainfield, New Jersey
One week later

Toro Borrono clenched his cigar so tightly between his teeth he nearly cut it in half. He pulled the broken thing from his mouth and set it on the ashtray.

Across his desk, Johnny Handsome sat roughly back in the chair.

"It's not as bad as it looks, Poppa."

"The fuck it isn't."

"Tony went rogue. You know, on his own. He's not family. They can't put this on us."

"Rogue? As if you didn't know nothing about it?"

"That's what I've said. That's what we've all said. That's what we're all gonna keep saying."

Toro shook his head. He took a deep, smoldering breath as he regarded the still smoldering cigar beside him, watched the ash grow.

"You make sure of that. Now get the fuck out of here."

He put his hands on his forehead and squeezed hard as the door shut behind his son.

The ash broke and fell across his desk.

"Marie!"

A muffled thump outside and Marie scurried in, head bowed, dressed in that little black and white maid's number that seemed to drive Johnny wild.

"What, you trip over Johnny on the way in?"

The knife was in his throat before Alena raised her head. Her apron was covered in blood.

Toro's hands reached out, but his strength, his own blood, was already draining away.

"You're son's dead, Uncle Toro. I wanted you to know that before you died. And one other thing..."

Her colorless eyes looked into his fading ones as she slowly twisted the knife.

"I don't work for you. I never did."

THE END

Other Titles by Steve Zell

Please visit: www.talesfromzell.com

TRUE CREATURE A series of suspicious deaths draws investigative reporter Deanne Mulhenney and medical examiner Sara Poole into a deadly clash of modern and ancient worlds.

"Zell's fans will want to grab this one, and new readers of his work will be entranced by his settings, people, and most of all his eerie, unchained true creature."
– *Feathered Quill Book Reviews.*

"10 out of 10. Reading this book is as entertaining as watching a film. Powerful prose and strong characters make this supernatural mystery a satisfying read and a page -turner."
– *BookLife Prize*

RUNNING COLD *"You soared like a rocket, or you blew up. You and everything, everyone, around you."*
In the hands of a young boy, an ancient gift can be a nightmare…

"A smart, smoothly written horror tale in the King vein."
– Kirkus Reviews

"Think of the King classic Stand by Me (The Body)… You'll need to sleep with light on for more than a few days…"
– Feathered Quill Book Reviews

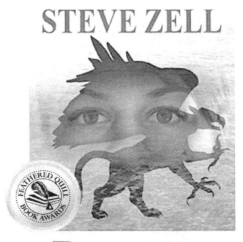

WiZrD It was a town that died with a powerful ancient secret. Now Piñon Rim is ready to live again.

"A perfect 50 out of 50 – this author knows his stuff and delivers great stories. The author's ability to draw strong characters must have given him a legion of fans already."
– Feathered Quill Book Awards

"Hair-raising. Fast-paced… with exceptionally well-drawn and engaging characters."
– Publishers Weekly

"Filled with slow- building horror."
– Kirkus Reviews

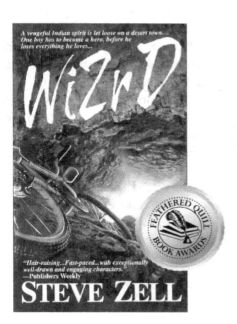

URBAN LIMIT "A move from the city to a new home in the mountains becomes a fight for survival for an Oregon family in this thriller."

"An unnerving but memorable tale that leaves myriad lingering questions for a pros-pective sequel."
— Kirkus Reviews

"Steve Zell delivers an edge-of-your seat, page-turning thriller in his latest novel, Urban Limit. Well done Mr. Zell. I look forward to your next thrilling tale."

— Feathered Quill Book Reviews

About the Author

It's been a twisted path… As a kid in Arizona, Steve Zell spent many days exploring the abandoned hotels and stores in then ghost town, Jerome. Even then he loved to tell ghost stories, draw scary pictures, and sing.

Set to study veterinary medicine at the University of Arizona, he instead became the editorial cartoonist for *The Tombstone Epitaph,* spent four great years performing with the *Invisible Theatre*, won two vocal scholarships, and wound up being UA's first Interdisciplinary Studies graduate. His major fields of study were Journalism, Studio Art, Vocal Production, Acting, Fencing…and Chemistry. You might think sharing a dorm room for two semesters with a Forensic Pathology Major who worked nights in a morgue would have soured Zell on the subject of medical examination…but, well, not quite…

Moving from Tucson to Los Angeles, his rock star dreams never did quite come true, although you may have heard his voice on various commercials as well as film and Soap Opera themes. Perhaps not surprisingly, he became the "Voice of Doom" for the series, *Baywatch* – singing sad rock ballads written by the writing team of Robin and Judithe Randall over any scene that featured a lifeguard having a really bad day…or dying.

Zell also spent several years as an animator and animation/FX tools instructor for the studios. Moving to Oregon to work at Intel Corporation, he started the Intel partnership with DreamWorks, and along with friends and colleagues Denise Gronewald and Wayne Ahrendt, co-founded the *Intel Audio Alliance*, a group of notable audio engineers, musicians and actors including George Massenburg, Allen Sides, Michael Boddicker, Graham Nash, Nathaniel Kunkel, Rory Kaplan and Billy Bob Thornton.

MANTIS

CPSIA information can be obtained
at www.ICGtesting.com
Printed in the USA
JSHW050707310521
15217JS00008B/5